Jump Start

A Novel

by

Gary Carter

PUBLISH
AMERICA

PublishAmer
Baltimore

First printing

ISBN: 1-4137-0193-0
PUBLISHED BY PUBLISHAMERICA, LLLP
www.publishamerica.com
Baltimore

Printed in the United States of America

ACKNOWLEDGMENTS

To Terry Baldino from Death Valley's National Park Service for his insight on Death Valley fossils, or rather the lack thereof, and to my family for their support over the years. Also to all the agents who rejected Jump Start's manuscript but left their little bits of wisdom on how to improve it. To Rose Stadler for her web site *the Write Mind* and her monthly words of wisdom for new (as well as "Old") authors, and finally to PublishAmerica, for taking a chance.

DEDICATION

To NANCY,
For all the great years.

PROLOGUE

SILENE, LIBYA
Circa 300 AD

Tired and blood spattered, George rode his steed through the blackened forest toward Silene. Behind him sat the Princess Alcyone, her hands and arms about his waist, her head upon his shoulder. Dragging behind, and tethered to the horse, came the skewered head of the Dragon, its huge, yellow eyes open and lifeless. Soon the weary duo reached the outskirts of town, there to be greeted by Silene's survivors, wildly cheering, glad to be free of the scourge that had plagued their countryside for years. Moments later their king had joined them, working his way forward with the help of numerous guards and courtesans. He greeted first his daughter, overwhelmed that she was still alive, and then George.

"It is done, then?" he asked, looking to George and the princess.

"Yes, sire," the handsome knight answered, dropping the tether and rubbing his arm. "Let us pray to God almighty that this is the last of them."

"There are others?" the king asked, weary also, the fear and loathing he had harbored for so long numbing his heart yet again.

"I have heard rumors," George answered, too tired to dismount. Despite seeing her father, Alcyone clung to her hero, not wanting to let him go. "They say that in China a few yet fly, and a stray one or two still terrorize both England and the Balkans. But it is merely rumor. To tell the truth, sire, I had never much believed in Dragons until venturing into your town."

"Well, you have need to doubt no longer," the king said, his eyes searching the skies, then returning to gaze at the Dragon's head. It was so much bigger than seen from a distance, and quite handsome in its own way. He felt almost sorry for it, then quickly squashed the feeling.

How could he feel sorry for a beast that had forced his people to live in fear and all but destroyed his kingdom? Thank God George had arrived when he did, Alcyone placed upon the sacrificial alter just that morning, the last of the town's children.

"I wonder where they come from?" George asked, looking around at the scorched earth and the small town, all but destroyed. "What manner of creature is it that possesses such a black heart and foul mind? It is as if they were spawned elsewhere, not of this world."

Chapter 1
Death Valley, CA
Present Day

JACOB MALFUSCO HELD ON AS HIS RED TOYOTA PICKUP steered itself up a steep incline. No sooner had he gained control than he was sliding sideways into a mesquite-filled ravine and losing his grip again. Once at the bottom he manipulated the wheel, stomped on the gas pedal and gunned the truck up the other side, finally leveling out.

"Geez," he muttered to himself, pulling to a stop on the rocky plateau. Jacob wiped his brow. Not because it was hot. It wasn't. He was sweating because he'd lost control more than once on the winding, narrow, seldom used road.

Jacob sighed and turned the engine off, then surveyed his old hunting grounds. *This could be it, old boy,* he thought to himself. *If you come up dry this time, you might as well end it.*

Jacob's head turned as three worn SUV's, an old VW bus and a battered Chevrolet truck came to a sliding halt behind his Toyota. He took a deep breath, trying to calm his jangled nerves and get into the spirit of the thing. The winter rains had been abundant and Jacob viewed the valley as few had ever seen it; green and lush and beginning to burst with what promised to be a spectacular spring. Even the ancient lake bed far below was full, close to overlapping the highway in several places.

Jacob pulled a bag of Frito's from the rear of his Toyota and ripped it open, watching as his students exited their vehicles one by one and stretched. He began eating, the start of what would be an orgy of junk food until the trip was over. Balding, overweight and pushing forty-five, Jacob didn't give a damn how he looked since his wife had died. Fact was, the only thing Jacob cared about now was his career, and he was fast losing interest in that. He had contributed nothing of importance to the university in close to a decade, and the patience of the powers that be was wearing thin.

Jacob continued to stuff his face until a skinny, blond, nineteen-year-old sauntered over and stood by his side, hands in the hip pockets of her tattered blue jeans. "It's beautiful here!" she exclaimed. "I thought deserts were arid, ugly places."

"It is pretty wild, isn't it?" Jacob said. "Unfortunately, young lady, it doesn't last long. Nothing does. Another month or so and all of this will be gone as the valley begins to warm up. Another two or three and the temperature will be in the hundreds. It won't look like grasses and flowers ever grew here, or ever could."

The girl smiled and surveyed the valley. Kim loved Jacob, as did all his students. He had a great sense of humor, was always helpful and never arrogant. Kim was soon joined by the rest of the party, twenty-four undergraduates out of San Diego State, all taking Jacob's paleontology class as an elective. Jacob, a botany professor with a passion for fossils, had long ago talked the dean into allowing him to conduct the class once a year. Paleontology, as a major or a minor, was otherwise not taught at the school. Hundreds elected his class, but few were chosen, a testament to Jacob's popularity and his teaching ability.

Jacob watched his class familiarize themselves with their surroundings. From their high plateau they could see the entire valley and the snowcapped peaks surrounding it.

"So, why did we nearly kill ourselves coming all this way?" Jacob asked his class. "Anyone?"

One of the male students gave Jacob a curious look. "To look for fossils."

Jacob nodded. "And, what kind of fossils?"

A short, redheaded girl raised her hand. "Any kind."

"Right you are," Jacob said. "And why's that?"

"Because no fossils have ever been discovered in Death Valley," the girl answered. "But we're going to change that."

"Ah, I like your thinking, Roberta. Anyway, the fact than no fossils have been found in the valley makes our hunt all the more interesting. If we do find something maybe we can put a lot of old myths and theories to rest. Does anyone remember what specific fossils we hope to find?"

"Pterosaurs," a brunette with pigtails and freckles answered. Her smile was bright and enthusiastic. "And pterandons! Large, flying reptiles that were believed abundant during the Cretaceous period. Some of them had wing spans up to forty feet!"

"And I like your enthusiasm, Janet," Jacob said, smiling her way. "Why do you think we might find them here, in Death Valley?"

"Well, it's an ancient lake, and this area dates way back. There was abundant water here during the Cretaceous, and, where there's water, history tells us there were animals. Dinosaurs, if you will, on which the pterosaurs fed. And the birds inhabited most of North America. Several of their skeletons were found in Big Ben National Park, in Texas, in 1975. More recently they've been found around Los Alamos, New Mexico, relatively just east of here. It is the professor's belief that they roamed as far west as California, and that's why we're here, to prove the professor's theory!"

Jacob broke into a broad grin. "Wow! You people have learned your lessons well. For your bonus you can take the rest of the day off. We'll get started first thing in the morning, after breakfast. As you know our permit gives us until the twenty-fifth to camp here. That's three days. We ought to come up with something by then."

You hope, Jacob thought to himself.

* * *

Jacob slept fitfully. The wind kicked in after the sun went down and howled all night. Temperatures plunged. Around midnight, unable to sleep, Jacob heard a couple making love in the tent next to him. He thought of Maria, and how god awful long it had been since he'd made love. Since losing her his only goal in life was to find some pterosaur bones somewhere in the vast southwestern deserts. He'd been searching close to fifteen years now and had never come close. He was feeling old, and losing interest in the chase. Maybe it was time to give it up, to pursue something else. Rekindle his interest in plants, take up golf, anything. Then maybe his colleagues at State would quit ridiculing him.

By three in the morning Jacob had decided that, if this trip proved as fruitless as all the rest, he *would* call it quits. Not since he was twenty-eight and had found a new species of chrysanthemum in the San Bernardino mountains had Jacob published anything worth reading. His career as a botanist had long ago dried up, and his career as a paleontologist had never gotten off the ground. He was tired of trying, tired of the hunt. Jacob was tired of everything.

He fell asleep an hour before it was time to get up.

* * *

On the second day, towards dusk when a cold winter sun was beginning to set behind the Panamints and the air was taking on its customary evening chill, Jacob's oldest student, a forty-two-year-old grandmother of three, made the find. At the bottom of a sharp, boulder-strewn ravine, about a hundred feet or so above the ancient shoreline, Sandi spotted a large, curved piece of bone protruding from a bank where a landslide had recently occurred. Jacob and the rest of his students scrambled, stumbled and slid down to the site. Excited, they looked things over.

"Looks like a rib," Jacob said, his heart pounding as he tried to balance himself on the steep bank. "Great job, Sandi," he said, enthusiasm for life suddenly returning. "Just a super great job!"

After an hour's careful work Jacob and crew had uncovered most of the bone, some fifteen feet long and curved like a new moon.

"Definitely a dinosaur rib of some kind," Jacob said, trying to catch his breath. He pulled an open bag of peanuts from his coat pocket, dumped some in his mouth and began chewing. His thoughts were always clearer when he was eating, or so he thought. "Look at the size of the damn thing!"

"Doesn't look all that old," one of his girls, a scholarly type wearing huge eyeglasses, said. "And look here," she continued, running her fingers beneath the bone, "there's still some skin left on it. Feels like skin, anyway."

Jacob scrutinized. "Strange," he said. "Maybe it's not a dinosaur after all. Could be a mammoth bone, or something else that roamed around here. Can't be too old, not with skin still clinging to it."

"Weird looking," the girl said, having pulled off a piece. "Never saw any skin that looked like this. It's more like a piece of, well, scale. Like fish have."

"Could be a new species," Jacob said, trying to solve the puzzle, as were his students. Visions of fortune and fame flooded his mind. His heart continued to race. He threw a last handful of peanuts into his mouth and chewed vigorously. "You know, like I've told you before, most scientists believe that only one percent of Earth's fossilized plant and animal remains have been discovered to date. That leaves a whopping ninety-nine percent not found. Things that inhabited our world way back when, or more recently, things that we've never seen or heard about, never dreamed of. Maybe we have something new here. Now, wouldn't that be something?"

"Cool," several of his student's said, catching their professor's excitement.

* * *

On the fourth day, after Jacob had gone to the Ranger Station with his discovery and received an extension on his permit, he and his students continued to work at the site. Clouds were scudding by overhead, blotting the sun out on occasion, making the day colder than the previous three. Despite the chill Jacob and his class had long ago shed their coats and sweaters. Moving yards of dirt was proving to be no easy feat, but no one was complaining. No one complained that the single bone was turning out to be part of an enormous, complete skeleton, either.

"Is it a pterosaur?" Kim asked around noon, caught up in the excitement of the dig. "Have we really found one?"

Jacob shook his head and took an oversized bite from his candy bar, then wiped at his brow with a soiled handkerchief. Despite losing sleep he felt good. Jacob found the exercise of climbing up and down the hills, along with the digging and the clean desert air, invigorating. He took another bite of the Snickers, sucked in a deep breath and spoke.

"I don't think it's a pterosaur, Kim. Not like any I've seen anyway. It can't be. The wing structure appears similar, but pterosaurs didn't have tails to speak of, and they definitely didn't have four legs to go along with the wings. To be honest I don't know what the hell this thing is. I've never seen anything like it, and neither has anyone else I know."

"Any ideas?" one of the young men, almost as rotund as Jacob, asked. Jacob's group of wide-eyed students looked at him expectantly.

"People, you may think I'm crazy but what I think we've uncovered here is the key to several thousand years worth of mythology and fairy tales," Jacob answered. He scratched at his head with a shaking hand. Everything fit. The wings, the legs, the long tail, a reptilian like head with razor sharp teeth, the talons. After all these years Jacob felt that, one way or another, he was finally going to be one very famous, and hopefully wealthy, man.

"Young citizens," Jacob continued, unable to keep his heart from racing. "I believe what we have uncovered here is nothing other than the well preserved bones of a long dead *Dragon!* Hallelujah!"

Had Jacob and his students any idea of the history behind their discovery, the joy they felt would have been short lived, soon to be replaced by a cold, heart-stopping terror.

Chapter 2
Ayers Rock, Australia
Early March

MARSHA KIMBROUGH PITCHED HER TENT AND LOOKED around. The view of Ayers Rock from this distance was incredible, but she was too tired to appreciate it. The long, boring drive down from Alice Springs had worn her out, and it was hot. Suffocatingly so. Summer in the Australian outback was no picnic, she'd heard, and so far the statement was proving to be more than true.

"What now, Mom?" her daughter, Tricia, asked. Tricia had graduated UCLA last June, happy to get her degree in archaeology and follow in her mother's footsteps. Marsha, who taught archaeology at the university, had meticulously planned her sabbatical so that Tricia might travel with her and begin her postgraduate work. Part of Marsha's life-long dream revolved around coming to Ayers Rock and studying the prehistoric drawings there. She had made it her life's work trying to tie the mysteries of the ancient world to alien astronauts, as many others had tried to do before her. It was her driving ambition, her one true belief. And now she was here. A few final links and she would have proof positive for her skeptics. She was sure of it.

"Well," Marsha answered, wiping her brow with the back of her hand. She sipped at one of the local brews she had brought with her, trying to cool off. "It's too late to go over. I think we should just take it easy the rest of the day. It'll be dark soon, anyway, and I'm bone tired. How about you, sweetheart?"

Tricia, a tall, slender, striking brunette, contrasted sharply with her mother who stood five-foot three, sported red hair and weighed close to 160 pounds. Their flashing green eyes were the only physical attributes they shared, other than a keen intelligence and a ravenous appetite for things supernatural and as yet unexplained. Marsha, though still quite attractive, was overweight by a good thirty pounds, and had been so for some years now, ever since the divorce.

"Fine with me," Tricia said. She looked off towards the world's largest rock, only half a mile or so from their camp. Because of Marsha's status as

12

an archaeologist, she and her daughter had been granted a campsite away from the usual throngs of tourists that haunted the Rock this time of year.

Tricia could not believe her eyes. The monolith, better known to the locals as Uluru, was more magnificent than she had ever dreamed. The planet's largest rock mass stood an impressive 1142 feet high and stretched for about 1.5 miles along its length. It stood out from the surrounding flat countryside like a huge loaf of eroded bread. Not tired at all, Tricia was anxious to get started on her Master's thesis, but knew her mother was worn out. Being overweight and drinking all the time didn't help. She could wait until morning. It would be cooler then, and they would get an early start on their explorations. Hopefully before the noisy and bothersome tourists got out of bed.

The girls cleaned up as best they could and then sat around their campfire for a while, drinking and talking in hurried voices about the coming day. They were going to collaborate on a paper. Marsha was particularly interested in drawings she had seen, from various books, that depicted what looked like ancient astronauts on the walls of Uluru. To her, at any rate. Stick figures with halos around their heads, other things that didn't seem to be from this Earth. She had ideas that her colleagues considered extremely radical and unbecoming a full professor, but Marsha was persistent and hoped her visit to the Rock would help tie some loose ends together. She was counting on it. Her and Tricia's paper could well lay to rest all the ridicule and scorn she had suffered at school over the years.

After a spectacular sunset, in which Uluru changed from tones of brilliant red to deep purple, Tricia helped her mother into her sleeping bag. She had drunk too much again, becoming inebriated. Tricia worried for Marsha. Her drinking hadn't lessened since the divorce. Instead it had steadily increased over the years. Her mother hadn't published since the separation, and was under the gun at UCLA. Tricia was going to help her get back on track, help her get started writing again. What had started as a brilliant career had failed horribly. Marsha had been prolific in the early stages of her work, making some astounding discoveries at Petra and Chichen-Itza in particular. Her mother had gone on to publish several well received books on her findings. All were standard college texts even now, despite her fall from grace.

Damn you, Dad, Tricia muttered as she fluffed a pillow for her mom. *Damn you all to hell for making her life such a mess.*

* * *

Around midnight the wind picked up and began a high-pitched, mournful wail. Gusts began topping out at over 100 MPH. Desert oaks were uprooted, tents ripped apart and hurled across the flat lands. RV's and fifth wheels were toppled. The majority of people left their campsites and cowered either in the stone-walled rest rooms or concrete supported Ranger Stations. Those that didn't suffered severe consequences.

Tricia rolled out of her sleeping bag around two, during the height of the storm. Fighting sand and dust she managed to move their rented van between the direction of the wind and their tent, saving their camp from being whisked away to some god forsaken stretch of the Outback. Much to Tricia's annoyment her mother snored blissfully through the whole thing.

The wind died soon after the sun came up, a brilliant ball of red-orange rising in the east. Marsha was up and about, cooking breakfast, bright and chipper and anxious to get the day going. Tricia was the tired one now, having enjoyed precious little sleep during the storm.

"Sleep well, darling?" Marsha asked at one point. Tricia could only shake her head in wonder.

They decided to walk the mile or so to the Rock. The morning was cool and most of the dust had settled out of the air by eight. The wind damage was considerable. All about lay flattened trees and scrub. Nestled up against the base of Ayers Rock were sand dunes that hadn't been there the day before. Off to their right, about a half-mile or so from camp, the girls could see where some, if not all, of the sand had originated. A huge, bowl shaped depression now lay where there had been but flat waste-land the day before.

"My oh my," Marsha said, straining her eyes. "That must have been some wind to do that."

"Told you, Mom," Tricia said, irritated. "Want to take a look?"

"Sure. Why not?" Marsha answered. After breakfast the two women gathered the things they would need for the day, confined them to backpacks, shook the bugs and grit out of their sleeping bags and then headed towards the depression. About half way there they saw a small pyramid sticking up from the middle of the bowl. Its color was that of gold, and it sparkled with brilliant pin points of light wherever the sun touched it.

"Must have been buried," Tricia said as she and her mother picked up their pace.

"No duh," Marsha said. "You can be positively brilliant sometimes, sweetheart. You'll fit right in at UCLA." Tricia ignored her.

Several minutes later, having reached the perimeter of the newly scoured basin, both women stared down in awe. Beneath the six-foot golden pyramid lay three other stones, equally gilded, each perfectly formed and sloping downward at the same angle. The sides facing the sun were so bright the girls had to shield their eyes from the glare. The triangular cap stone measured an even six feet from top to bottom, corner to corner. The stones below were half buried in the sand.

"Trish, are you thinking what I'm thinking?" Marsha said, her mind unable to comprehend what her eyes were seeing. Her heart pounded unreasonably and she found it difficult to breathe. After several minutes of openmouthed awe, she and Tricia made their way towards the object. Half way down the bank, Tricia trailing, Marsha pulled a small flask from her hip pocket and took a swig, wincing as the fiery liquid made its way to her stomach.

Tricia didn't answer. Angry at her mother for drinking so early in the day, she opted to keep her opinions to herself. Once at the bottom she gingerly slid a hand up and down a portion of the heavily pitted, metallic surface. "What do you think it is?"

"I know what it is," Marsha said, not without arrogance. "God knows I've seen enough of them." She stepped back and once again shielded her eyes. "It's the top of an Egyptian pyramid, Tricia darling, only this one's not in Egypt. Why it's here, and how it got here, I haven't a clue."

* * *

Three weeks later, after the authorities had been notified and the site thoroughly excavated, the girls stood on the rim of a one mile square pit. They stared in disbelief along with thousands of other people from all walks of life, the majority of which were media types, scientists and tourists. The noise surrounding the pit was deafening. Overhead airplanes, helicopters and hot air balloons fought for space. Down below, sandwiched between the cranes, earth movers, bulldozers, police, construction workers, stadium lights and a thousand other things in the hole was an almost perfectly preserved, three hundred and four foot tall pyramid. By the time the proper tests had been run the structure was found to date back approximately 9,000 years, the oldest structure of its kind ever found.

The Kimbroughs had plenty to write about. The whole world wanted to know what was going on, especially since there was no record of any pyramids having been discovered in Australia. Papers and magazines from around the globe clamored for Marsha and her daughter's attention. The girls were almost positive the pyramid was linked to some Aborigine paintings at Uluru they believed depicted ancient astronauts. They also believed the Dragon inscriptions they'd found somehow tied in with ancient myths and legends.

Everyone listened but nobody heard.

Chapter 3
Mount Palomar, California Five Months Later

PAPALOV ULYSSES DARRINGER, his heart pounding, moved as fast as his sixty-eight-year-old legs would carry him. Tall and frail, with bushy gray hair, mustache and beard, he limped down the steps that led away from the observatory. A golden-red sun was rising over the desert to the east and the sharp scent of pine needles and sage brush filled the air. Somewhere a crow scolded, but Papalov hardly noticed. He was late for his own meeting, not a good thing to be for the senior astronomer on the mountain.

Another fifty feet along a cobbled walkway and Papalov pushed through a set of double doors and hurried inside. Jabbering away the Nobel Prize winner shuffled down the sparsely furnished hallway to a meeting room he had helped design and fund. Papalov turned around and backed through the door, the door that had "DARRINGER HALL" emblazoned over it in blue and gold. On entering the room he fumbled, then dropped the papers, photos and graphs he had been carrying. Nonplused, the aging scientist gathered them up then shuffled over to a worn podium situated in front of a long hardwood table. There he put his notes back in order. That done he looked up and smiled at his bored and bleary-eyed associates gathered around the table, a few sitting straight, some with chins in hands and others with heads flat out on the table, eyes closed. The time was five-thirty A.M., but Papalov had called the meeting for five. His associates were not happy, but they were not unhappy, either. The doctor was usually late but, on the rare occasion he *was* on time, *you* had better be there. Besides, they all loved the old man, and he did sign their paychecks.

"Good morning, everyone," Papalov began, looking at his notes. The aroma of freshly brewed coffee permeated the room, but again the doctor failed to notice. Besides, he'd already consumed more than his usual quota of caffeine, having been up all night at the observatory checking and rechecking his photos and calculations. He ran a long fingered, bony hand through his unkempt hair, absentmindedly trying to straighten it. He fumbled with his too large glasses and crumpled tie. Papalov was nervous about the news he was about to deliver, and he had every right to be.

"Sorry I'm late," he continued, "but I have important information that concerns all of you. I'm sure you'll all agree, once you've heard it, that it was well worth the wait."

Papalov's associates certainly hoped so. It was Sunday morning, after all, and most of them had gone to bed late. A few of them had drank too much and were now paying for their indulgence. Most were on their second or third cups of coffee or tea, and as a group they were wondering why in the hell their chief had called such an early meeting, especially since it was Sunday, and everyone's supposed day off.

"And what news would that be, boss?" one of the women associates, in her mid-thirties and quite attractive, asked without enthusiasm. Even though she had worked with the doctor for almost twelve years now and was used to his hastily called meetings, Margie was not really interested in anything astronomical this morning. Where she wanted to be was where everyone else wanted to be, and that was home in bed.

Papalov turned around and began posting photographs on the peg board behind him. In his haste they continued to fall almost as fast as he pinned them to the wall. Finally, with help from several others, he had them where he wanted them. Once his sour-faced helpers were back in their seats Papalov returned to the podium.

"You will recognize these photos as pictures of the Orion Nebula," he said, facing his audience, even though the photos were too far away for them to see clearly, especially with red eyes that refused to focus. "Yesterday evening, after you had all gone home, I discovered what appears to be a massive meteor shower headed towards Earth from that direction. Needless to say I haven't slept since. According to my calculations they will strike our world in less than a year. That's why I've called you all here so early, we've got a ton of work to do. If my figures are correct, and I have every reason to believe they are, then our very selves, and the world as we know it, could cease to exist in the near future."

Everyone's eyes popped open at the same time, including Margie's. People began talking to one another. While science had been predicting just such a catastrophe for decades, none of them wanted to hear it, no one wanted to die. On the other hand, nothing of any consequence had been discovered out of Palomar for some time, so the news generated mixed emotions.

A wizened, silver-haired astronomer, on sabbatical from England, cleared his throat and spoke from the back of the room. "Why do you say 'appears to be?' Dr. Darringer? Meteors are meteors, aren't they?"

"Yes. But there seems to be several million of them at this point."

"Several million? That's ridiculous, isn't it? I mean, to the best of my recollection nothing like that has ever been encountered before, has it? So many, all together?"

"Those were exactly my thoughts when these things were first encountered, Harold. Then I got to thinking. There are millions of asteroids in the asteroid belt, and millions of rocks, pebbles and other debris in Saturn's rings, so why not millions of meteors? I think what we're seeing here are the remains of an exploded planet, or something similar. Something odd about this swarm, though."

"And what's that, Pappy?"

"Well," Papalov began, "they all appear to be about the same size, Harold. In fact, if my preliminary measurements are correct, they *are* all the same size."

"But, how can that be?" Margie interrupted. Brows around the room creased as everyone's eyes focused on Papalov.

"Exactly what I was wondering," Darringer answered.

Chapter 4
San Diego, California
Early October

"... and so, ladies and gentlemen, that's how we found George, the world's first honest to goodness Dragon," Jacob Malfusco finished. He smiled at his audience and finished off his can of Jolt. His stomach growled and he realized it had been an hour or so since he'd had anything substantial to eat. Tired, he took in a deep breath and surveyed the spacious, circular room, a sparkling new addition to the Natural History Museum in Balboa Park. Heavily polished oak benches sat atop a red brick floor in straight rows. Spanish tile decorated the walls, and there was even a marbled fountain in one corner. All for him and George. Outside a steady rain was falling and a moderate wind was blowing palm trees and other tropical plants about. A beautiful, lazy, fall day in a city known for her abundance of beautiful, lazy days. Overhead George's skeleton hung from the ceiling. His wing tips all but touched the many windows lining the circular walls of the building. He looked menacing and formidable, even without his skin on.

"Are there any questions?" Jacob asked, and fifty hands shot up simultaneously. They always did. No one could get enough of George. Jacob sighed.

"Have they decided on a scientific name yet?" a young woman, who had jumped up from her chair in the front row, asked without being recognized.

Jacob frowned. "No, not yet," he answered, overcoming his irritation. "The committee is still kicking things around. It's a brand new taxon, and there's a lot of red tape involved. George's DNA, and a few other things, are proving a little strange, but that's to be expected of an entirely new species of animal. There's still a lot to be tested and, of course, a lot of people are convinced George is nothing more than an elaborate hoax. But we know better, don't we?" Jacob concluded. He winked at the young woman, who blushed and sat back down.

"How big is it?" a young boy of fourteen asked from the middle of the room, also jumping up. He glanced at the massive overhead creature, completely in awe of the winged terror, as was everyone else in the overcrowded room. Built to seat one hundred, Jacob guessed there were at least an extra fifty people lining the walls and crammed in the doorways. The museum was obviously raking in the bucks. People came from all over the world to see George. Chinese, Japanese, down-unders and up-overs. Which was good, seeing as how Jacob received twenty-five percent for each seminar he gave. Now at the height of his newfound career, Jacob was rapidly becoming a wealthy man, not to mention a living icon.

"How big is what?" Jacob asked, not liking the inference to his discovery as 'It.'

"George. The Dragon," the boy answered, confused at the question and Jacob's hostility.

You need a day off, old man, Jacob thought to himself, seeing that he had frightened the boy. He forced a smile and answered the question.

"George's wing span measures approximately fifty feet from tip to tip, much larger than any flying reptile, or bird, ever found," he began, pointing an arrow towards the ceiling, at George's relevant structural components. "The body proper measures close to forty feet from head to tail. The four legs, as you can see, end in talons and are similar to an eagle's feet. And the head, well, it's kind of like a cross between an alligator and a T-rex, wouldn't you say? George was definitely a ferocious predator, unlike anything this old Earth has seen before or since. At least so far. Who knows what we'll discover next week, right?"

"Er, yes sir," the boy said, not looking up from the notes he was scribbling. Then, quickly, before anyone else could interrupt: "You said the bones were hollow?"

"Yes, like a bird's. George had body scales, too. Tough but light. We found quite a few of them, currently under analysis. The wings, tail, tail flipper and skull crest are framed in bone and covered in something similar to leather, only lighter, thinner and much tougher. And, in case you're wondering about the whale-like flipper, it measures about twelve feet across and was in all probability used in aerial maneuvers. It was a steering device, along with the crest on George's head. We have to believe he was the most agile creature to ever inhabit Earth's skies, even for all his size."

"You keep referring to George as 'He'?"

Jacob shrugged. "Obviously, we don't know. Not yet, anyway."

"Thanks," the boy said, then sat back down and continued to scribble. He was no sooner seated than a dozen other people were up. Jacob rubbed tired eyes and popped another can of Jolt. He threw a handful of Corn Nuts into his mouth, chewed vigorously, then downed them with his beverage. Towards the back of the room stood a woman Jacob thought he recognized. He had never met her, but he had seen enough of her pictures and was flattered she was in the audience. Jacob wiped his mouth, pointed her way and nodded. Marsha Kimbrough kept her feet while the others, disappointed, sat back down.

"How do you account for the fact that George has four legs?" Marsha asked, in town for some lecturing of her own. Though somewhat overweight Jacob thought her quite pretty, and he thoroughly enjoyed talking to pretty women now that he had his new found status. "Along with two wings? That's six appendages! Unheard of among the vertebrates."

"We can't," Jacob said. "And paleontologists as a group are divided on the issue. What I can say is that we believe only one percent of Earth's historic flora and fauna have been discovered so far. That leaves a whopping ninety-nine percent still to be found. Maybe the next thing we'll find will be fairy bones, or the Loch Ness monster. Who knows?"

"According to what I've read George is only nine thousand years old. How do you account for that? I thought dinosaurs were millions of years old?"

Jacob cleared his throat. "We can't account for that, either, but we do have some theories. Our best explanation, one I have advanced, is that George is a relative of the Dragons we find in all our ancient literature. As you probably know Dragon myths and fables abound in mankind's early history. Indeed, even in our later history. In Europe, the mideast, India, China, Japan. Even here, in the America's, in the form of Quetzacoatl, the feathered serpent, whose head resembles a Dragon. But why? Why are Dragons so prevalent in our literature? Why do we find them imitated all around the globe? Because *they were real*! George's discovery has explained a lot of old fables, just as some of the old Bible stories are now being explained as new evidence is presented," Jacob said, beginning to ramble. He continued, his speech becoming a well rehearsed monotone. "As you may recall George was named for Saint George, who supposedly slew a Dragon to save a town. We can now presume that the story had some basis in fact . . ."

"But then, if they were so prevalent, why haven't more fossils been found?" Marsha interrupted, peeved at her questions being pushed aside.

"I believe I already answered your question, Miss . . . ?"

"Kimbrough. Marsha Kimbrough. Then you really believe that?"

"Really believe what?" Jacob asked, becoming irritated with the questions.

"That Dragons originated on Earth!"

"Well, there's your proof," Jacob said, pointing his arrow at the ceiling.

"But your Dragon has six appendages! You're not listening here. No animal on Earth has six appendages, Professor. Who did George descend from?"

"From other Dragons, I would suspect," Jacob said dryly. "What's your point, anyway?" he asked. Heads twisted back and forth, glancing expectantly from Jacob to Marsha and back again, enjoying the argument.

Marsha, eager to expound her theory in front of so large an audience, was quick to respond. "There are some who say George came from outer space, brought here by alien astronauts come to visit. He, and perhaps a few others, which would be a better explanation of his being found on our planet."

"And I'll just bet you're one of those 'Some,' are you not?"

"Well, yes, as a matter of fact, I am," Marsha answered defensively.

"And *you* really believe *that*?" Jacob patronized. A ripple of laughter spread through the audience, irritating Marsha even further. Jacob had heard the argument before, of course. It was common enough. But no one had ever posed that particular theory to him at one of his seminars. Jacob found himself at a loss for words.

"Yes, I do," Marsha said, defiant and self assured now. "Think about it. Your Dragon is nine thousand years old, hardly a prehistoric creature. That's about the time mankind got started, isn't it? Jericho in Israel, Catal Huyuk in Turkey, Damascus in Syria, Knosos in Crete. I believe all these cities got started around 9,000 BC. People in China came together about this time and initiated communal farming in the far east. Other places are suspect for earlier construction dates. Stonehenge, Mojenjo Daro, Cahuachi in South America, close to Nazca, a small pyramid there before the lines on the mesa were ever drawn. Tiahuanoco in Mexico. The list goes on. The pyramid at Uluru. No one has a clue to who built that one, and it also dates back to around 9,000 BC. And don't forget the Dragon inscriptions at its base, almost identical to the ones on the Ishtar Gate in old Babylon. Doesn't it strike you as odd that all of humanity got its start around the world at about the same time? Maybe *the* same time? Maybe these Dragons in our lore were alien pets, and some of them escaped, or were left behind for whatever reason."

"You're telling me you think that my Dragon, Dragons *per se*, were tied in with ancient civilizations? Come on," Jacob said, finding it hard to keep from laughing at Marsha's proposal.

"Isn't that what *you* just said?"

Jacob flushed. "Yeah, but what you're saying is a little far out, don't you think? I mean, astronauts at Jericho and Stonehenge and all?"

"You don't seem to have the answers," Marsha countered, pushing her advantage.

"No, I don't," Jacob said. He fought to compose himself. Draining his can of Jolt he surveyed his audience, everyone on the edge of their seat, staring his way, looking for answers that he didn't have. All of a sudden he felt drained, and queasy. His head hurt. Someone had pulled the plug. Time to go. He gave these seminars twice a day during the week, except Tuesdays, and four times daily Saturday and Sunday. He was tired. Tired of the questions, tired of the speculation, tired of trying to figure out what the hell *was* going on. He had never dreamed that fame and notoriety could wear a person down so quick, not to mention all the hubbub and stress that had gone into building the museum and getting George set up in the first place. If this was what it took to become a celebrity, Jacob decided, he wanted no more part of it. Not today, anyway. He looked towards Marsha, still waiting for him to reply. Jacob decided to bail out.

"People, I'm sorry, but I have to be elsewhere pretty soon," he lied, glancing at his watch, "so I'm going to have to cut the question and answer portion of this lecture short. If any of you would like to come back tomorrow, go to the cashier's booth and I'll see that you get free tickets. I bid you all good day, and you might want to consider Miss Kimbrough's idea. At this point in time it's about as good as any," he finished, though Jacob, personally, had never believed in ancient astronaut theory.

Over groans from his audience Jacob gathered up his notes, then hurried off the stage and into the crowd before anyone could object to the rude way he had ended his seminar. They had all paid their ten dollars, after all. He ran to where Marsha was still standing, an angry look on her face, and stood in front of her.

"You left me standing here looking like an idiot," she spat, confronting Jacob. "What the hell was that?"

"Look, I'm tired, and I *don't* have all the answers. I came over to apologize. I'm sorry. I really am. Your questions threw me off guard and a sudden urge to run overwhelmed me. Please. I'm sorry."

Marsha looked him over. Now that he was closer he wasn't all that bad looking. Overweight by quite a bit, but so was she. And about her age, too. Marsha took notice that Jacob wore no wedding ring. Hmm. Her anger began to dissipate. He had apologized, after all. Curious, she waited for him to continue.

Jacob took a Nutty Buddy from his coat pocket and bit into it, then offered the bar to Marsha. Disgusted, she frowned and refused, waving the candy away with a shaking of her hand. Jacob couldn't help but notice how her silky, auburn hair washed over her shoulders as she moved her hand. Up close he thought her quite beautiful, and amply endowed, the way he liked women to be. Jacob jerked the candy bar away.

"Are you who I think you are?" Jacob asked out of the corner of his mouth, wishing he hadn't bitten into the bar. Jacob took a step forward, his body drawn towards Marsha. Marsha took a step backward.

"And who might that be?" she asked, still looking the taller Malfusco over. He was no prince, but she was taking a liking to him. Kind of like her, in a way. She chewed on her lower lip for a second, then smiled, something she hadn't done for a man since her divorce. Not the kind of smile she gave him, anyway. It had come naturally, and it surprised her.

"*The* Marsha Kimbrough. You're the lady who discovered the pyramid in Australia, aren't you?" Jacob asked, running his tongue around his teeth, trying to clean them.

"Yes. My daughter and I happened to be someplace at the right time. For once. Like you."

"I read your book. I'm not sure I agree with your conclusions, but I enjoyed reading it. Pretty wild."

Marsha lost her smile. "No one asked you to agree with it."

Jacob frowned. "Listen, are you doing anything?" he asked tentatively, shoving the unfinished candy bar back in his pocket.

"Well, no," Marsha answered, caught off guard.

"Good. Would you, well, would you like to get something to eat? I know a great little restaurant up the road. They serve Mexican. We could talk about things. Please? Let me make up for my rudeness."

"Well, I *had* hoped to ask a few more questions."

"Great! I promise to give you my undivided attention."

Marsha pursed her lips and looked Jacob over again. She certainly didn't like his attitude towards her work, but then she was used to that. And she *was* hungry. She was *always* hungry.

"There *were* Dragons at my pyramid, and they did look similar to those in Babylon."

"I know. I saw the pictures."

"All right," Marsha said, her stomach growling. "But only for dinner."

Jacob smiled. "Follow me," he said. He took Marsha's arm and escorted her towards the door. Outside in the showroom a small line had formed at the cashier's booth. Some of the people looked angrily at Jacob. He instructed the person inside the booth to issue them free tickets. He would pay for them. Once that was done Jacob smiled at his fans and then escorted Marsha out the front door, noting that the rain had stopped. A tropical breeze hurried through the trees and grass. Jacob's headache vanished. He felt good, and his hand felt good on Marsha's arm. Best of all, she hadn't objected. It had been a long time since he'd held a woman's arm. A very long time. And such a pretty arm, too.

Jacob and Marsha turned down the street and, unknowingly, headed into a world that would soon find them, and everyone they shared the planet with, running for their lives in a world gone mad.

Chapter 5
One Too Many

Marsha was breathing heavily by the time they reached the restaurant.

"I thought you said it was just up the road?" she pouted, upset at Jacob's hurried pace.

"Sorry," Jacob apologized. It was a thing he did, walking extra distances, moving about at a fast pace, getting up and down to change TV channels instead of using the remote. Little things to try and get some exercise, to try and keep his weight down. He should have been more considerate, especially as she was wearing high heels. Jacob took Marsha's arm again, she having pulled it away some distance back, when the pace became too hectic. Jacob proudly escorted her inside the restaurant. "I hope you like Mexican," he thought to ask, after the fact.

"Love it, " Marsha said, catching her breath and thoroughly enjoying the Spanish architecture and decor.

Jacob had a petite Hispanic waitress seat them outside, beneath a large orange and white umbrella, at a beautifully decorated wrought iron table overlooking a large spouting fountain surrounded by colorful marigolds and petunias. Old, gnarly eucalyptus trees and tall palms swayed beneath a cloudy sky while doves and pigeons strutted about the fountain, cooing, fighting, taking baths and searching for handouts. The early evening air was fresh and invigorating, washed clean by the earlier rains. Marsha, who had never visited Balboa Park before, fell in love.

"It's gorgeous here," she gushed, taking it all in.

"Glad you like it," Jacob said, pleased that Marsha was pleased. And, although he hadn't planned it, he was overjoyed at the romantic fireworks the surroundings were setting off.

Jacob ordered a Corona for himself and, at her request, a strawberry margarita for Marsha. She downed it in one gulp. Curious, Jacob ordered her another and then the two of them dove hungrily into the salsa and chips provided. They soon discovered they had at least one thing in common: a healthy craving for food and drink.

After another round of drinks Marsha, feeling no pain, disclosed that her husband had left her five years ago, for a younger woman.

"He said I was getting fat, and that I was never home. I was giving too much time to my career and not enough to him. Hell, he was never home either. The bastard!"

Out running around with other women, Jacob surmised, but he didn't say that. It was obvious to him from the start that the ordeal had taken a great toll on his dinner companion. When she had talked her way through it, Jacob told his story.

"I lost my wife two years after we married," he began, a far away look in his eye. "An accident on the freeway. One of those things you read about but think will never happen to you. Some drunk crossed the center divide and hit her head on. It's been almost twenty years now. We were both starting our teaching careers. No kids, although we desperately wanted them. Just a lot of love, hope and dreams."

"That's quite a bit," Marsha sympathized, "when you think about it."

"I suppose you're right," Jacob said, despondent. "It didn't seem like much at the time."

"The best things seem like the least because they don't cost anything. Hopes and dreams are life's sunbeams, Jack."

"Right again," Jacob said, tipping his Corona to Marsha. He finished it off, ordered another. What the hell. He wasn't going to let a woman drink him under the table. Marsha finished her third margarita and ordered a fourth, along with a fresh bowl of chips.

"I'm sorry you lost her," Marsha said, beginning to feel the effects of her drinks. She scrutinized Jacob again over the rim of her glass. He didn't have much hair up top but she could live with that. Despite her vows she was starting to like the guy, and she wasn't sure if it was because of the margaritas or simply because he was a guy. "You never remarried?"

"No time. I kind of drowned myself in my work for a while. Still do. Especially now. You know the story."

"All too well."

The two shared each other for a while, making small talk, their eyes darting back and forth, each afraid to connect with the other. Overhead the clouds had begun to dissipate and the stars were coming out, making for a grand evening, even if a bit cool. Jacob pulled his coat tighter and Marsha her sweater. The waiter finally showed up and they ordered dinner. One good thing about Mexican, Jacob mused, was that it was relatively cheap. With the way his date was chug-a-lugging her drinks it was making for an expensive evening.

"They called me 'Malfunction' in high school," he said, after their orders had been placed.

"Malfunction?" Marsha giggled.

"Yeah, for Malfusco. I was kind of a nerdy type guy. You know, read a lot, didn't go out with girls, got good grades, didn't play sports. Not much, anyway. I was on the baseball team, but second string. Never got to play, even though there were only twelve of us. I'm still not sure the Malfunction tab was on account of my personality or the poor way I played. Probably both."

Marsha laughed. "They called me 'Kimbrat'."

"Kimbrat?"

"Yeah. My parents were wealthy. I was the only kid in school who drove a Mercedes and ate out all the time. I was an only child. Spoiled rotten."

Now it was Jacob's turn to laugh. Caught up in each other they made small talk until their orders arrived. Jacob had ordered a full plate, Marsha a taco along with beans and rice. For some reason she had decided to go on a diet. Both ate tentatively at first, then dug in, their hearty appetites overwhelming their manners. Both scientists and now famous, they had a lot in common, a lot to talk about. After a while it was almost as if they had known each other all their lives. Once the meal was over Jacob ordered coffee and dessert, Marsha yet another margarita. Over cake and ice cream Jacob finally summoned up enough courage to ask the question he'd been wanting to ask all evening.

"I gather, from your books and you questions, that you truly believe in extraterrestrials?" he said, sipping at his cream and sugared coffee.

"Yes. And I gather you don't?"

"No. Sorry."

"Then I'll ask it again: how *do* you account for George?"

"What do you mean?" Jacob asked, dreading another argument.

"You find what you call a Dragon in the middle of the desert? Come on. I thought Dragons lived in Europe and Asia, places like that."

"Apparently they lived in America, too. George is the proof. And besides, have you ever heard of Quetzacoatl?"

"The feathered serpent of Central America?"

"That's the guy. My colleagues and I believe his legend has been passed down from antiquity, long before the Mayans and Incas ever existed as tribes. We believe their forefathers encountered Dragons, when they first migrated to America. There's Dragon-like stone heads all over Central America."

"Then what happened to them? You're saying George is 9,000 years old, or something like that. If Dragons are that young they should still be around, shouldn't they? I mean, like elephants and crocodiles and such?"

Jacob shrugged. "Would you like another drink?"

"You're evading my questions again."

"What was the question?" Jacob asked, stalling for time. It was obvious Marsha was becoming upset again, and he didn't want that, not with the evening going so well.

"Let me rephrase it," Marsha said, becoming woozy from her drinks. She put her Margarita down, set it to one side. "Where are the Dragons now? I mean, 9,000 years ago is pretty recent for a species to die out, isn't it?"

"Mammoths died out only ten or so thousand years ago," Jacob said defensively.

"Yes, and because they are so recent, we have an excellent fossil record of them! That's exactly my point. Where are all the Dragon fossils?" Marsha asked, then belched. Embarrassed, she drank some water.

"I just found it. In the desert, remember?"

"You'll have to do better than that to convince me, Mr. Malfunction. One Dragon does not a species make. At least not an Earthly species, and especially not one with six appendages."

Jacob winced. The woman certainly was persistent, and he had to admire that. "All right, I'll do my best. I believe George was a relic. Relics are species that exist in small pockets hare and there, leftovers from another time. We have them now, all over the world. The Grizzly bear in Alaska, the Arctic wolf, the desert pup fish. The Torrey pine, right here in San Diego. Species of plants and animals that once existed on a much larger scale but are now narrowed down to only a few locales. It's my belief that George was the last of his kind, or close to it. In America, anyway. He died when the lake dried up and there was no more food. Time will tell. Dragons in mythology have never been numerous. One here, another there. I think they were on the brink of extinction when man began coming out of the bush and settling down. No doubt we helped in their demise, being the great and ruthless hunters that we are. I think they died out after men began writing history. Saint George may have indeed slain the last of them."

"Go on," Marsha said as Jacob paused to take a breath. "I'm not sure I'm following you here."

"What I'm trying to say is I believe Dragons as a species were dying out as man was coming on. They were around before we began recording history.

Confrontations all over the globe, and these became legend, passed down from generation to generation by word of mouth, then glorified when man finally began writing stories. George and his ancestors finally died out for the most part, say around the time we began building our first cities. I don't know why. These were huge animals. They would require a great deal of food to keep them going. There's been plagues and famines all through human history. Why not Dragon history? Maybe they starved to death, or, like I said, maybe we hunted them out of existence."

"Then why have there been no Dragon bones discovered in prehistoric caves?"

"You mean in the garbage piles?"

"Yeah."

Jacob shrugged again. "Be tough to carry a Dragon back to your cave, don't you think? Who knows? There's lots of unidentified bones sitting in museum rooms all around the world. Maybe if they're sifted through again we might find some. Anyway, that's my theory. There are lots of mysteries surrounding Mother Earth. Sudden die-outs abound. The dinosaurs. Neanderthal man. The woolly mammoth. And no one has solved those dilemmas. Not yet, anyway."

"So you're saying Dragons were in abundance at one time, then died out about the time humans were getting on their feet?"

"Yep. It's the only thing that makes sense when you put two and two together."

"What about the six appendages?"

"Insects have six appendages."

"You're saying Dragons and insects are related?" Marsha asked, an incredulous look on her face. Then she burst out laughing.

"Ever hear of the dragonfly?"

"Give me a break," Marsha said, continuing to laugh.

"Look, if you believe in evolution then you believe we all descended from the same organisms way back when. Who's to say there's not a whole line of Earthly animals yet to be discovered, animals with six appendages! And we've just discovered the first one. Is that so far out?"

"It's not far out at all, Malfunction. If you listen to yourself, it's downright ridiculous!"

"All right. You think it's ridiculous?" Jacob asked, feeling his anger build and not wanting it to. "Then let me hear your theory, Kimbrat. The one about ancient astronauts and all that, that . . ."

"Crap?"

"You said it, I didn't."

Marsha cleared her throat and fought at cobwebs forming in her head. "I think George and the others came along with the astronauts, since you ask. I think we, as humans, were jump started on the road to civilization. Like you said, George dates back to the time when men were starting to build cities and tame the land. But think about this. Long before George died strange and good things began to happen around the globe. Not just mud huts and caves, but pyramids, Stonehenge, Easter Island, Nazca, Glozel in France. You know the names."

"Yeah, I know the names. But those places are hardly 9,000 years old."

"We don't know for sure, Jackson. Dates at archaeological sites are always being pushed back."

"Yours is not a new theory, you know," Jacob said, trying not to antagonize his new friend. Never in his life had he believed his planet was visited by aliens and he was surprised, and disappointed, that a scientist of Kimbrough's stature could believe in such things.

"A whole lot of folks believe we've been visited by aliens," Jacob continued, finishing off his coffee. "I won't argue with you there. There's certainly a lot of unexplained phenomena in this world. And I agree to a point. How did the Egyptians and Mayans build those colossal pyramids? What about those batteries in Iraq? But how does my George fit into all that? And by the way, it's Jacob, not Jackson."

"I already told you," Marsha said, having trouble keeping her composure. She hiccupped. "The aliens brought them along as pets. Or maybe guardians. You know, like pit, pit bullsh."

"Those are pretty damn big pit bulls!"

"Look, if you're going to swear, then I'd just as soon go home," Marsha said, becoming angry at Jacob's attitude towards her work.

Jacob glanced at his watch. It *was* getting late and he had to be at the museum at eight A.M. for his first seminar. Not only that, it was obvious to him, and everyone around, that his dinner date had been drinking too much. Way too much, apparently. But Jacob had to have the last word.

"Look, I'm sorry I swore," Jacob persisted when he should have shut up, "but, you know, the idea of Dragons as pets doesn't set quite right with me. Sorry again. Anyway, I can see I've upset you. If you want, I'll take you to your car."

"Maybe they rode around on them. You know, like in the Dragons of

Pern? Those kinds of shtories," Marsha countered. "Kind of like we ride horshes." She picked up her empty margarita glass and tipped it onto her lips, as if there were something still in it, then sat the glass back down and wiped her mouth with the back of her hand.

"You're telling me you actually think your aliens rode Dragons around?" Jacob said, and he couldn't hold it in any longer. He began to laugh. He laughed so loud and so hard that other patrons on the patio looked his way, perturbed that he and Marsha were making so much noise.

"You eat too damn much, you know that?" Marsha said, wanting to change the subject, wanting to hurt Jacob as much as he was hurting her, the way everyone hurt her when she talked about ancient astronauts. But it all fit! Why wouldn't anyone listen?

"I'm sorry?" Jacob winced, Marsha's words having their desired effect.

"I said you eat too damn much!" Marsha shouted. She stood up, wiped her mouth with her napkin and threw the soiled cloth onto her plate.

"Now who's swearing?" Jacob said, equally loud.

"Never mind! I'm ready to go."

"All right, all right," Jacob said, embarrassed. "Calm down."

"And don't tell me to calm down!" Marsha said, then whirled and staggered back inside the restaurant, towards the front door. People looked at Jacob and shook their heads, silently admonishing him for letting his woman drink too much. Jacob left a hundred dollar bill on the table then took off after Marsha, afraid she might walk off a curb and fall down or something.

"Wait a minute!" Jacob yelled, catching up to Marsha after she had weaved her way across the road. Jacob caught her arm as she slumped onto a Spanish style wrought iron bench, out of breath.

"Shtay away from me," Marsha said weakly. She pried at his hand but hadn't the strength to dislodge it. The way her eyes and head rolled Jacob could see she was close to passing out. "You're jush like all the rest."

Jacob, still holding on, gently pulled Marsha to her feet. Once up Marsha looked at Jacob with disgust and managed to find enough energy to jerk her arm away. Then she began zigzagging down the dimly lit walkway. Jacob had to grab her arm again and turn her around as she was headed in the wrong direction.

"Keep your hands off me!" Marsha hissed, but made no effort to pull her arm loose this time. The two of them made their way east beneath swaying palms and a star-studded sky. Jacob put his arm around Marsha's waist and held on for dear life, afraid his date was going to collapse at any moment. A block away from their cars Marsha had to sit down. She couldn't walk any farther. Jacob hurried and got his car but by the time he returned Marsha had passed out on the bench, her head resting on a plastered Roman column. With the help of a passerby Jacob managed to wrestle her into his car. Marsha never stirred.

Jacob, winded from the ordeal, started his car and, with some misgivings, headed north.

"You can sleep it off at my house, all right?" Jacob said, talking to his sleeping companion, Marsha being slumped over next to him in the front seat. "I live just over the rise there, in Mission Hills. You can sleep it off at my house. And I promise to bring you back to your car first thing in the morning. How's that?"

Marsha snored her consent and Jacob drove on, windows down. His mind contemplated how he was going to haul Marsha up the two flights of stairs that led from the alley behind his house to his back door. No doubt he could find out where she lived by the contents of her purse, but he couldn't take her there like this, could he?

Jacob sighed and drove on, driving past houses and apartments and tall eucalyptus trees. He had sure screwed this one up. And what would the neighbors do if they saw him dragging a body up the back steps? Call the cops?

Chapter 6
Doomsday

Jacob parked his car in the garage and got out. Luckily no one was about. No kids playing or folks strolling along the tree lined alley. But then it was late, and a school night. Overhead a full moon had risen and the air smelled extra sweet after the first rains of autumn. Jacob, feeling invigorated despite the situation, took a deep breath and bent to the task at hand.

Arm wrestling Marsha out of the car he managed to drag her up the twenty steps to the back door of his three-story home. No way was he going to bring her in the front, even though the door was a mere fifteen feet from the curb. Not in her condition. Not with the gossipy neighbors he had.

Jacob's house stood in a fine, older neighborhood of San Diego, up in the hills northeast of the bay. He had bought it many years ago when prices were much cheaper, an older home in bad need of repair. He and his wife had used their meager savings and borrowed from his parents to make the down, then Maria had died. She had loved the house, as he had. Nothing fancy. A downstairs, partitioned basement, a main floor with living and dining room, a kitchen and a single bedroom and bath off the dining room. An upstairs single room. Small, but perfect for them. They would add on as the children came along. Expand the upstairs, further partition the basement. A perfect home in a perfect neighborhood in a perfect town to raise their kids. Now Jacob used the room upstairs as a study, and the basement to cram all his junk into, which was considerable. He had thought of converting it from time to time. But into what? He had left the many small rooms alone all these years, watching in dismay as they slowly became littered with the refuge of age. Now he rarely went down there, and then only to store more junk and his camping gear. Or more food, water and supplies for the inevitable, catastrophic earthquake. Jacob, paranoid about possible disasters, was prepared for the worst. Besides, there was always the possibility he could lose his job, though that was a remote possibility now that he had discovered George.

Jacob finally managed Marsha into the living room, having to drag her up another flight of stairs from the basement. She came to for a few seconds as

Jacob was lying her on the couch, then quickly passed out again. The room was warm so he left her without a blanket. While moving about he couldn't help but admire her ample figure. Not bad. Not bad at all. The thought flew through his mind to take advantage of her, it had been so long, but that wasn't him. He was content to look, and hope, even after the disaster at the restaurant.

Jacob turned the TV on low and quietly opened the windows. The room smelled of stale cigar smoke, peanuts and beer, all of which Jacob loved to consume as he watched TV. Not that he did much of that lately, what with the book he was writing, his teaching at State and the museum and all. There was barely time to sleep anymore with his busy schedule.

He retrieved a can of pine scent from the kitchen cupboard and sprayed it around the house, most of it in the living room. A cool, ocean breeze began making its way through the many open windows. Jacob hurried to cover Marsha with a ragged old beach blanket he kept in the closet. It was all he could find. Some of his plants had wilted so he quickly watered them, apologizing as he went along. He had over thirty of them, hangers and uprights alike. Every nook and cranny in his home was adorned, where there was enough light, with one or the other. They were good companions who didn't talk back or scold. Being a botanist Jacob harbored many rare and exotic plants among his collection. He couldn't wait to show Marsha.

If she would only stay awhile in the morning.

Once everything was watered he opened the front door and let his three cats in, all of whom had been yowling since he'd gotten home. Jaws, the old, mangled, orange Tom, a huge cat, by anyone's standards. Maws, his black and white neutered female who could never get enough to eat, and Paws, the white, long-haired junior of the bunch at seven years, whose feet were much too big for his small frame. They scrambled over each other to get in the house, then, smelling something new, ran over each other in getting to the living room. Arranging themselves by the couch they scrutinized Marsha and, finding themselves jealous, scampered back into the kitchen. There they growled their displeasure at Jacob, then hurried back out the still open door, turning their collective noses up at the gourmet food Jacob had dished out for them.

"She's not staying!" he yelled after them. "So don't get all bent out of shape!"

Jacob, amused, followed them out and lit a cigar. Vintage Havana, now that he could afford it. He gazed at the moon and stars for a while, asking them questions as he puffed away, content for the moment. Then he grabbed a bottle of Dos Equis from the kitchen and went back into the living room. Marsha was still out, snoring peacefully. He would wake her in the morning and take her back to her car. Hopefully she wouldn't remember too much of their later conversation, when they had argued. He wondered if she drank like that all the time, or only because they had been together, and she had wanted to enjoy herself, wanted to unwind. Jacob hoped it was the latter.

He pulled one of his chairs closer to the TV so he could hear it, just in time to see a distraught Papalov Daringer come onto the screen. Jacob recognized the man as someone who had been in the news lately. The astronomer was talking to some high profile talk show host, Jacob couldn't remember his name. As the camera angle shifted Jacob saw another five men and two women in the room, all seated, questioning Darringer. Each of them, including the host, wore agitated, concerned expressions. Jacob nudged his chair a bit closer and turned the volume up a notch.

" . . . our best estimate is that they'll be here within four or five months," Papalov finished saying.

"Why have you waited so long to warn everyone?" a middle aged, scholarly looking woman asked. "It's our understanding you've known about these, these asteroids, or whatever, for some time now."

"Since August," Darringer said awkwardly. He fiddled with his glasses. "Actually, they're meteorites. Millions of them. Too many to count. The biggest swarm mankind has ever seen, at least so far as we know. Maybe the biggest in the universe. It wasn't until a week or so ago that my colleagues and I were sure they *were* meteorites. Not that it will make much difference."

"What do you mean by that?" a distinguished looking man of around sixty asked.

"When I first discovered these things I thought it might be a large asteroid, perhaps even a small planet. The entire mass is much bigger than anything you've seen on TV, or speculated at. An asteroid of this mass could conceivably split the Earth in two. We doubt these meteors can do that, but, even so, after they've impacted it's not likely anything will survive."

"You're predicting doomsday," the man said. Others leaned forward, scrutinizing Darringer. Papalov fiddled with his glasses again.

"I don't see any way around it. There are so many. We can try all the scenarios. Launch missiles, load up our shuttles with nukes, whatever. But there are just too many. We can't hope to eliminate but a fraction before they hit. Not with our present resources, anyway."

"Not with all the Earth's peoples pulling together?" the talk show host asked.

"I'm afraid not," Papalov answered, leaning awkwardly in his swivel chair.

"I understand the government asked you not to come here," a serious looking, younger man asked. Jacob recognized him as America's latest billionaire. Some intellectual, computer whiz-kid not yet thirty. The young man reached over and steadied Papalov's chair, afraid the elderly doctor might fall out of it.

"That's correct, Mr. Markham," Papalov answered, having forgotten the kid's first name. "They're afraid of a world wide panic. My own feelings, and that of my colleagues, are to inform everyone. We think it better to let the world know, so that they might enjoy the last days of their lives doing what they want to do, rather than have everyone stampeding each other at the last moment."

"Jesus, you're serious about all this," one of the men said, then cradled his head in his hands.

"Rocket ships to other planets?" the host asked.

"Too late, I'm afraid. Governments of the world, ours in particular, have known this could happen at any time. God knows there's been enough movies and documentaries made on the subject. Scientists have been predicting just such a catastrophe for close to half a century. We should have had colonies on the moon and Mars by now. NASA has been begging for decades, but it seems our governments prefer war to anything worthwhile. I hate to be the bearer of such dreadful news, but we think it's best everyone knows. It is our opinion, I'm afraid, that the human race has precious little time left." Papalov stopped and looked into the cameras. "To those of you watching," he said, an ominous tone to his voice, "you need to make plans."

"What sort of plans?" the scholarly woman asked, the beginnings of tears in her eyes.

"Well, we can't run anywhere," Darringer answered, his eyes coming back to his audience. He rocked back and forth, bit at his nails. "There are so many meteorites that we believe they'll be bombarding Earth for days, if not weeks. Coming down all over as we rotate. There's no place to hide. You might be able to survive in a cave maybe, or an underground bunker. There will be tidal waves, so those along the coast may want to move inland. Even if you do survive the onslaught there will be the nuclear winter we've all heard so much about. There's not much room for miracles, I'm afraid."

"Armageddon," a sober Father Rochelle, seated across from Papalov, said.

"You said these meteors were pretty much all the same size?" the host asked, ignoring Rochelle's comment. "How is that possible? I mean, I thought meteors came in all shapes and sizes?"

"They do," Darringer said. "It's my feeling that what we're seeing is the remains of an exploded planet or moon, possibly a large asteroid. Over time, crossing space, the different sized blocks would rub and knock against one another, eventually grind one another down, kind of like grains of sand on a beach. Something like that. Right now we have no other explanation."

"This is not some wild hoax?" a stern looking lieutenant general, decked out in full military dress, asked. "Somebody's idea of a sick joke?"

"No, General," Papalov answered, avoiding the man's eyes. "We wish it were. This information has been verified by astronomers around the globe."

"And we have only five months?"

"At the most," Papalov answered. "Right now the storm is coming our way from the constellation Orion. It's heading on a course that will bring it close to Jupiter. At this point Jupiter is some 484 million miles from earth. Unless their speed changes they'll be here around March."

"Jesus," the man who had his head buried in his hands said again. He dropped his hands and stared at the floor, too stunned to look around. The group sat silent for a while, the implications of what Papalov had said slowly sinking in. Even the usually vociferous host was quiet, at a loss for words.

"Then there's no hope at all?" the other woman, a striking Asian lady in her early fifties, asked after a few minutes, breaking the silence.

"There is one hope," Papalov said. He stopped rocking, sat up straight, cleared his throat. "As you know, recent theory has it that Jupiter, along with Saturn and Neptune, have acted as shields for the inner planets since our solar system was born. In 1994 the Shoemaker-Levy comet broke up and plummeted into the atmosphere of our giant neighbor before it could impact any of the inner worlds. Jupiter's gravity is so strong it has the power to do this. As I said, the trajectory of the meteor swarm will bring it close to our huge neighbor. We believe, we hope, they'll be traveling close enough to be sucked in by Jupiter's gravity. Right now that chance is looking better and better."

"When will this occur?" Father Rochelle asked as sighs of relief spread around the room. Rochelle crossed himself, then gazed at the ceiling and said a silent prayer as Papalov answered.

"Within two weeks."

"What are the chances?" the host asked, glad that his show was not going to end on an entirely sour note.

"Fair to good. We're hoping most of the meteors will be pulled into the well. Any stragglers, hopefully only a few, shouldn't pose any major problem to our planet. However, this is something new, and as scientists we've come to expect the unexpected. It's possible Jupiter's gravity may have little or no effect on the swarm, therefore we advise everyone to be prepared for the worst," Darringer said. He leaned sideways in his chair again. This time he wasn't so lucky. His chair spun and several glasses of water were knocked off the small table and onto the floor.

"And pray," the Father said, bending over to help clean up the mess.

* * *

Not quite believing, Jacob turned off the TV and went into the kitchen. There he retracted a bottle of scotch and a large glass from the cupboard. Next he filled the glass with ice from the refrigerator, poured scotch over the ice and went outside. There he sat on the back steps where he was soon joined by Jaws, Maws and Paws. Forgiving now, and hungry, they rubbed at his legs and purred, oblivious to the problems of man. Jacob lit a cigar, sat his glass down and gazed into the sky, at some secret place beyond the full moon and its halo of stars. A soft breeze stirred, bringing with it the sea-salt smell of the nearby Pacific.

"Why now?" Jacob asked of the heavens, ignoring his cats, the night and the breeze. "Why now, when everything seems to be going my way?"

Later, groggy with too much drink, Jacob snuffed out his third cigar and stumbled back into the house. He tiptoed into the living room, lay on the floor next to his still snoring guest, and promptly fell asleep. His three cats gathered about, still rubbing and purring and wondering where their usual late night snack was.

Chapter 7
Countdown to Chaos

Despite feeling as if someone had imbedded an ax in his brain, Jacob managed to wake himself up around six. Slippers on he staggered into the kitchen and got the coffee going, fed the cats and awakened his guest.

"Where am I?" Marsha said, bolting upright, frightened at her unfamiliar surroundings. Once Jacob had calmed her down he escorted her into his small dining room and sat her down with some coffee.

"Oops, forgot something," Jacob said, barely seated. Rising from the table he went into the kitchen and brought back a box half filled with stale, powdered, sugar doughnuts. Offering them to Marsha she stuck her tongue out and made a face.

"Get real, would you?" she said. "Yuk."

"I have instant oatmeal."

"No thanks. Coffee is fine. You want to tell me how I ended up here?"

Jacob sat down and, over coffee and several doughnuts, told Marsha everything. Her passing out, his bringing her home, the meteors, everything.

"You didn't do anything funny last night, did you?" was Marsha's response.

"Like what?" Jacob asked, his feelings hurt.

"What do you mean 'Like what?' You know what I mean."

It took several minutes for Jacob to convince Marsha he hadn't done anything. They discussed the impending meteor shower for a few minutes, then Jacob, trying to get back on Marsha's good side, made her a peace offering.

"Would you like a real breakfast?" he asked, hoping she might stay awhile. "You must be hungry, and I make a mean Spanish omelet. Toast, juice, the works. You name it, you got it."

"Why? So you can make fun of me all over again? Get a life. What I want is to use your bathroom. After that, you can take me to my car. And please don't smoke on the way. Your house smells like burned horse hair, you know that?"

And you smell like a brewery, Jacob thought, but bit his tongue.

"All right," he said reluctantly. "The bathroom's over there. I'll gather your things and wait for you downstairs."

* * *

Thirty minutes later Jacob deposited Marsha next to her Lincoln Continental. Luckily it hadn't suffered any vandalism, or been towed away. Jacob had exited his side and opened the door for her before she could protest. The morning was cool and quiet, most of the shops and museums not open until ten or later. Flocks of pigeons made their rounds, unaware of Earth's impending disaster. Jacob wondered if, after last night's news, the shops would open at all.

"Here," he said, once Marsha was in her car and had rolled down the window. He handed her a small, rectangular slip of paper.

"What's this?" Marsha asked, her reflexes grabbing the card before she could think about it.

"It's my business card. See the little Dragon in the corner? It's got my telephone number on it. I, well, I really would like to see you again. Will you call? Or give me your number?"

"Fat chance of that," Marsha said. She glanced at the card.

"Look, I'm sorry about yesterday. I really am. You're right, I should be more open minded. That's what science is all about. Give me a chance here. You and I, we have a lot in common. Maybe . . ."

"I don't think so," Marsha said, cutting him short. She turned to look up at Jacob. "I meet your kind all the time, Jack. Yours is the only explanation that is correct. You can't explain why it's correct, but that's okay. For your information, Malfunction, there are millions of people in this world who do believe in extraterrestrials. If you would sit down and think about it, really think about it, then you would see it's the only logical explanation for our past. Including your damn Dragon!"

"Look, Kimbrough, I said I was sorry. What do you want from me?"

Marsha handed the card back. "Something you haven't got, Jack. Now, if you'll excuse me, I have a long drive back to Santa Monica. I have a lot to do."

"You live in Santa Monica?"

Marsha ignored the question. Inserting her key into the ignition she started her car, backed up, pulled out and headed south. With a sinking heart Jacob watched her go. He pulled a cigar from his shirt pocket and started to light it, then changed his mind. Angry at himself and the way things had turned out he threw it into some bushes lining the sidewalk.

"Damn you, Jacob," he said to himself as Marsha's car disappeared down the street. "Damn you all to hell."

* * *

The news spread rapidly. What was once only hinted at had now become reality. People around the globe stayed tuned to the news, but few panicked. Most everyone went back to work. There was no mass buyout of food and water, no rush on generators or gas cans. Science had saved the day before, and they, along with massive Jupiter, would save it again.

Jacob would listen to the news on his lunch break, on his way to and from work and at home, same as everyone else, everywhere around the world. Every morning, noon and night, without fail. There were a lot of differing opinions.

"Papalov failed to mention," another astronomer said, "that, if the meteors do get past Jupiter, which now seems unlikely, then they will burn up in Earth's atmosphere, same as the smaller meteors have been doing since our planet was born. It will be a minor miracle if any of them strike our planet's surface at all. Things will heat up a bit, there may be some melting of the polar caps and the glaciers, but that should be about it. Nothing to worry about if you ask me."

"If they do make it into the oceans," another said, "there will be no tidal waves. Not disastrous ones, anyway. There are so many that the ripple effects will cancel each other out."

"There are just too many of them," other scientists rebuked. "Some of them are bound to get around Jupiter, and some of those will make it to Earth's surface, following on the coattails of others. Some of us will die. Perhaps many."

Jacob, like everyone else, didn't know who, or what, to believe. He added a few things to an already overloaded larder just in case. Candles, matches, another camping stove, fuel and a couple of blankets, canned goods, things he could use down the road if the meteorites never made it. He worried, but not a lot. Like the rest of the world he believed in science. He *was* a scientist, after all. And if you couldn't believe in your own kind, who could you believe? Jacob was firmly in the "Jupiter Will Take Them Out" camp. He had to be. The alternative was too frightening.

Exactly six days and seven hours after Papalov had shocked the world the entire meteor swarm split up and went over, under and around Jupiter. Following the news people around the world began to panic.

* * *

"What the hell was that?" one of Dr. Darringer's associates asked in the conference room at Mt. Palomar. "Jupiter should have pulled the majority, if not all, of those rocks in! Not one fell into the gravity well. Not one hit a single moon or its ring. Not one! That's impossible. It's against all the laws of physics."

"Physics as we know it, anyway," another associate said.

"And what the hell is that supposed to mean? A fourth dimension? Parallel universes? C'mon, Frank, this is bad enough without everyone going metaphysical."

"Please," Papalov said from behind his podium. He picked up a glass of water, dribbling some of it onto his shirt before getting it to his lips. "This isn't helping anything," he coughed, then choked as some of the liquid caught in his lungs. Finally, with the help of the two graduate students in the room, he quit coughing and regained his composure.

"It's as if something were guiding them," an elderly astronomer said from the back of the room. He ran a hand through gray hair. "They're too damned small to be spaceships, aren't they? My God, now there's a thought!"

"Guided missiles?" the Asian lady suggested.

"For Christ's sake, Lo Sing!" Frank said. "Three million guided missiles? What the hell is that?"

"Obviously our physics aren't quite up to snuff," a distinguished British astrophysicist, visiting the mountain, said. "Something we've bloody well missed, wouldn't you say? Somewhere along the line?"

"Jesus Christ," Frank said, shaking his head. "Now we're repeating ourselves."

Nobody had the answers. The only concrete thing about the situation was that the meteors were still on line to impact Earth. Hearts and minds around the room raced, trying to come up with something, burdened with an impossible task. According to that morning's calculations, the storm would strike in five months and twenty-eight days.

"All right, listen up," Papalov said, trying to keep order. "Here is what we're going to do. I want us all to go down the mountain and pick up provisions. Water, canned goods, food that won't perish. We'll make a list, and we'll use our research grant money. No one outside this room is to know the impact date. Not until we're all set here. We'll go to different stores in the off chance we'll be recognized. Once the impact date is announced the panic will only increase. It's going to be every man for himself in a matter of days, maybe hours," Darringer continued. He cleared his throat and began filling his glass from a pitcher of water, but found his hands shaking so much he couldn't finish. Embarrassed, he set the vessels back down.

"I'm sorry it's come to this," Papalov continued after placing his hands on the podium top. "You're all welcome to stay here, along with your families, or you're free to go once the provisions are secured. It's your call. We should be safe in the basements. At least until, until . . ."

Darringer found himself at a loss for words.

"But, what if one of the meteors impacts the mountain?" his female graduate student asked. Papalov noticed blood on her lower lip.

"Then nothing's going to matter, is it?" Papalov answered. "We'll never know what hit us, and maybe that's the way to go."

"We'll be living like bloody moles," the British astrophysicist muttered, wondering how he was going to get back to England and his family.

After a brief, somber discussion, the group made their joint list, adding here and subtracting there. Next they divided the list and went their separate ways, afraid for themselves, afraid for the world. None of them mentioned the fact that they were taking unfair advantage of their neighbors. At this point in time, and considering the circumstances, none of them really gave a damn.

* * *

That night the news spread around the globe. Humanity came to realize that their chances of surviving past five months were slim and none. Many panicked, but, once again, most remained calm, or tried to. They weren't going to die tomorrow, after all. With security forces out en masse order was kept. Families connected and made plans for where they wanted to die. After the initial shock wore off people went back to work. Except for the rich and well-to-do few people had enough money saved to stock supplies for five months anyway, had there been enough to stock. People still had to eat, and you needed money to buy food, and if you were a farmer or food processor you couldn't have food to sell if you sat home and cried about things.

And, besides, way down deep, most people still believed science, or God, or both, would save the day.

* * *

Two days after the announcement the governments of the world forgot their differences and formed a united front for combating the threat. Plans were drawn up. Remaining nuclear missiles would be redesigned to fire into space. Existing space shuttles would be armed and sent into orbit, there to wait until the swarm arrived. Earth's three space stations would also be armed. For those who would protect the world when the time came the plans were a clear suicide mission. No one believed Earth's orbiting battle stations could take out any but a small fraction of the meteors. But, it was a chance to go down fighting and, as time would tell, there would be more than enough volunteers.

The United States, with help from others, would reinstate the Apollo program, only on a much grander scale. Plans were drawn for colonies on Mars, as there was little doubt the moon would be obliterated along with the Earth. Still, the station being constructed there would be rushed to completion. As the moon virtually kept one side faced toward the Earth, perhaps the storm might impact the opposite side, and the colony survive. Another suicide mission, but another chance for man. Auto makers and other manufactories would retool immediately, using their knowledge and skills to put man into space permanently. The government of the United States made ready its armies to protect the colony launching sites from last minute hoards.

Life went on, but not as usual. People planned, and acted, and waited. They lived life to the fullest as best they could, straining schedules and budgets. It was a different time. People forgot their hatreds, prejudices and forgave former transgressions. Love blossomed and sex was never better, or more urgent, and to hell with contraceptives. Marsha Kimbrough called Jacob two weeks after the meteors had bypassed Jupiter.

"Can you come up?" she asked, straightforward as was her style, still wondering where she had acquired the courage. "I, I'm sorry for the way I acted, Jacob. You mentioned you lived alone? There's no one else?"

"Yes to both questions," Jacob answered, surprised and overjoyed. "Just me and my three cats, anyway." It had been a dismal four weeks. The museum had canceled his seminars due to lack of participation. To his dismay he and George were now all but forgotten. Jacob understood why, but that didn't help him digest the fact. His rise and fall in the science world had been quick, and precipitous. To hear Marsha's voice again quickened his heart and did wonders for his soul.

"I'm, well, I'm all alone, too," Marsha said, following a brief and strained silence. "And I've quit drinking, Jacob. Honest. I have. And I'm sorry I got wasted. Can you come up?"

"For how long?"

"For as long as you want. I, I've been on a diet, too."

"Can I bring my cats?"

"Yes. Of course. Bring whatever you want."

"Can I smoke?" Jacob asked, although he'd quit the morning Marsha disappeared over the hill.

"Yes."

"All right. The university is shutting down anyway. Last day is tomorrow, as a matter of fact. The students are leaving to be with their families, or sweethearts."

"Yes, I know. My daughter moved in with her boyfriend several days ago. They're still getting married next week, then off to Hawaii and to hell with the expenses!"

"I heard the banks and credit card people aren't lending money anymore," Jacob said.

"I know. My Tricia and her man had some money saved, and I gave them the rest. I, well, you can't take it with you, you know? If you need some, Jake, I have plenty."

Jacob had never liked being called "Jake," but, for some reason, coming from Marsha it sounded good, and reassuring, as if she had known him for a long time.

"No thanks, Marsha," Jacob said, speaking her first name for the first time. "I have some saved, too. Might as well spend it. It's getting to be Confederate money anyway."

"What's that? Confederate money, I mean."

"During the Civil War Confederate currency became more and more worthless as the war dragged on. I think ours is going to do the same."

"The government's backing the banks up, and they have safeguards against runs."

"It doesn't matter one way or the other, Marsha. Not if it's Confederate money. It'll be worthless pretty soon. Anyway, are you sure you want to do this? I can't guarantee anything."

"I'm sure."

"Then I'll see you in a couple of days. Once I have your address. And, by the way . . ."

"Yes?"

"Thanks for asking."

Three days later, his affairs in order, Jacob packed up what he could, gathered Jaws, Maws and Paws, said good-bye to his house and neighbors and headed north, towards Santa Monica. He was surprised at the heavy traffic on the freeway, almost bumper to bumper the entire way. The long columns of military vehicles didn't help matters any.

Chapter 8
Fire in the Sky

The temperature was above normal for March. Not only in Santa Monica, but all over the world. Even though the swarm was three days out, the heat generated from the sun's energy reflecting off its collective mass had raised Earth's mean temperature by several degrees. Night had ceased to exist. Only daylight, and dimlight, and strange shades of orange, yellow and gold existed to guide humans about. Terror gripped the world.

The nuclear missile plan had been scrapped. There was not enough boost to get them into space, and not enough time to get them enough boost. A greater fear than the meteors was that the missiles fall back upon the earth, ending life there once and for all. The space shuttle and space station plans had also been eliminated. The recoil from a single missile fired, no matter how small, would have knocked them out of orbit and sent them screaming back to earth, burning up as they entered the atmosphere. Instead their materials had been salvaged to finish the moon base and build three interplanetary spaceships. One had been used to carry a hundred and one men and women to the recently completed underground city on Luna. Calculations proved that the meteorites would indeed impact the side opposite of the moon base. Hopefully Earth's first space colony would survive. So far they were doing fine. Terrified, perhaps, but not as terrified as their counterparts on Earth.

Two Mars vehicles, carrying twenty-one passengers each, were on their way to the red planet, situated on the far side of the sun and well away from the oncoming swarm. The world had wished them God speed, and God knew they would need it. There had been little trouble at the launch pads. Those who went had been the best qualified to do so. One-third men, two-thirds women, an almost equal racial mix, intelligent, unattached and in their prime. There was hope on the moon, and hope on its way to Mars, and that would have to do. The vast majority of those left behind felt no ill will. By their way of thinking to die a quick death on Earth would be far better than a slow, agonizing one on two, far away, very hostile worlds.

As hope dwindled suicide rates across the continents steadily increased to thousands per day. Families and friends tried to hold each other together. Most people living along the coastlines of the world had moved inland, there to live with relatives or pitch their tents in makeshift camps alongside RV's, fifth wheels and cardboard shanties. Even now, as the massive swarm swung ever closer, tidal surges were several feet above the norm, and would get worse. To walk on a beach anymore, anywhere, was to invite almost certain death. Low lying coastal cities were inundated on a daily basis along with coastal tidelands, estuaries, sloughs and other marginal areas.

Work had ceased a short month ago. People, at least in the United States, had hopefully stored enough provisions to get through their last days. There was little panic. Instead, all around the globe, humanity had settled in, trying to make the best of their final days.

The Malfuscos stood in the dimlight, on the second story balcony of Marsha's home in Santa Monica, high on a hill overlooking the Pacific. They watched as a yellow sea danced beneath the winds of a spring driven storm. Overhead the heavens pulsed with a golden light that colored the stars and moon. Far off the horizon blazed, as if a new sun were being born. But it was a cold blaze, eerie and strange, a fire not of this Earth, but of something far away, unknown, and alien.

The newlyweds snuggled closer together, oblivious to the approaching storm as only newlyweds, deeply in love, could be. Jacob wrapped his arm around Marsha's waist and pulled her close, then nibbled at her ear. In an effort to please one another, coupled with the worldwide food shortage, they had both lost close to thirty pounds over the last five months.

"Mmmm," Marsha murmured, pushing into Jacob. "You can stop next week."

"There's not going to be a next week," Jacob said, then wished he hadn't.

Marsha looked into his eyes and frowned. "I thought we weren't going to go there anymore," she said.

"Sorry. It slipped out."

"Then don't let it slip, damn it!"

"It's really quite pretty, in an odd sort of way," Jacob said, after awhile, after he had summoned up his courage once again and quelled his despair. "Like living on another planet. The yellow sea and gold sky and all. Orange moon, multicolored stars, no nights. I can see what's coming. Newport and Long Beach and Venice are all under water, and I still don't believe it."

"None of us believe it. We're all in denial. That's the only thing keeping us from going berserk and killing one another. That and the hope the swarm will split up and go around Earth, like it did around Jupiter."

"Listen," Jacob said, tightening his grip around Marsha's waist, "I want you to know something. I'm glad you came into my life. These past five months, well, they've been the best of my life. If I have to die, this is the way I want to do it. In your arms. I never thought I could fall in love again. Thank you for making my life worth living."

"And you've been good for me too, Mr. Malfunction," Marsha said She turned and, standing on tiptoes, kissed her husband long and passionately, finally coming up for air.

"Wow," Jacob whispered. "Is that an invitation to go back inside?"

"You old devil," Marsha whispered back. She took his hand and led him of the balcony. "Can't get enough, can you?"

"No, ma'am," Jacob said, following diligently behind. "Not with you. You're quite beautiful, you know. Especially now, since you've, you've . . ."

"Lost weight?"

"Yeah."

"You need glasses old man," Marsha countered as she led Jacob into the bedroom. "But thanks, anyway."

* * *

Papalov Darringer stared out the conference room window and shook his head. It was nine P.M., yet it seemed like high noon. The forest fairly glowed, almost as if it were on fire. A heavy wind rippled the trees, causing them to emit a deep, soughing sound, as if they longed for the world they had once known. Papalov continued to stare, wishing the landscape would change back into the lush greens and deep browns he loved so much, but knew his wish to be hopeless. Nothing could save them now.

He shook his head forlornly and returned to the podium. He studied the notes and photos there as his colleagues looked on. Except for the Englishman, who had returned to the Isles, the rest of his associates, and their families, had elected to stay on the mountain. They were not alone as, several months before, the observatory had been assigned a Marine platoon out of Camp Pendleton, there to protect them and the facility should a miracle occur and riots ensue.

"Anybody have any comments?" he asked, looking around the room. "Any new ideas?"

"Does it matter?" one of the men asked, echoing the thoughts of the others in the room. "Even if we knew the answers, it's too late to do anything."

"I thought we agreed to keep trying until the countdown was over," Papalov said, then sighed. His eyes settled on his old friend, who turned and gazed out the window. The man was right, of course, Papalov realized. Had been for some time now, he and the others. Despite the situation the doctor kept calling the meetings anyway. It was his way of trying to keep his group together, of trying to maintain stability, and sanity. Still, by looking around the room, he could see that the rope that held them all together was becoming more and more frayed as doomsday approached. It could break at any time.

Maybe it's time for me to call it quits, Papalov thought to himself. *To give up, like everyone else.*

He was about to say the same when his male graduate student, who had elected not to attend the meeting, burst into the room. Gerald was breathing hard, and his face was flushed.

"What's the matter?" Papalov asked. "Has something changed?"

"The meteors, they, they're slowing down!" Gerald answered, choking the words out.

* * *

Five days later the Malfuscos stood on the balcony as the first of the meteorites entered the Earth's atmosphere, lighting up the sky in a blaze of yellowish-orange columns. Jacob and Marsha held their breaths and squeezed each other's hands so tight the blood all but stopped. Terrified, they wondered how much longer they had to live, and how painful their deaths were going to be.

Soon the sky was streaked and crisscrossed with a hundred-thousand fiery trails, lighting up the sky so brilliantly that the Malfuscos had to shield their eyes. With thudding hearts the newlyweds fell to their knees and held onto each other, having vowed weeks ago to meet this thing head on and get if over with. Marsha began to cry and Jacob pulled her as close to him as was possible, afraid to look, afraid to breathe, feeling the heat as the temperature around him began to rise. Seconds later the first wave of meteors struck the Pacific, far out and away, sending spumes of salty water skyrocketing into the sky. Then wave upon wave impacted, churning the surface of the ocean into a cauldron of boiling water.

The storm, expected to last for days, ended exactly twenty-four hours later, off the west coast of Mexico and South America, only miles from where it had begun. By the time it was over Earth's atmosphere had heated up ten or more degrees, generating typhoons and hurricanes all around the globe. When things calmed down twelve hours later it was learned not one of the shiny, smooth, oval shaped objects had touched down on land. More surprising, no lives, other than those unfortunate enough to have been on sailing vessels at the time, or caught in the winds, had been lost.

Chapter 9
Interlude

Five months is a long time to worry about when, how and where you are going to die. When the peoples of the world began to realize they would live after all a whole range of emotions swept over them, not the least of which were outright joy and hysteria. Confusion reigned. No one could explain what had happened, or what might happen next, least of all world and religious leaders. The President of the United States, once he had his wits about him, called a meeting of his staff, his top military officers and several prominent scientists forty-eight hours after the last meteor had disappeared into the Pacific. Those that he could find, anyway, considering the circumstances.

"Somebody want to tell me what the hell that was all about?" he bellowed, searching the White House conference room for answers. Jack Samuels was a big man, heavy set and in his late fifties, a product of a hard-knock ranch situated in the heart of the Oklahoma panhandle. At six-foot-six and two-fifty, not only was he imposing physically, he was a master politician possessed of above average savvy and intelligence. Samuels looked around the room, daring anyone to meet his baby blue eyes.

"All this crap about our planet blowing up," he continued, pacing up and down behind a solid oak podium. "All this BS about a nuclear winter. And, my God! The money we've spent sending people to the moon and Mars! Do you people know that as a nation we are bordering on bankruptcy? Do any of you care?"

Samuels continued to pace. He glared about the room, at the sixty or so people seated there, at the twenty-odd plus standing. Finally, hearing nothing, he came to rest behind the podium and challenged the room with his eyes. He needed answers, and he needed them fast.

"Doctor Darringer," he said, looking directly at Papalov. "You're the one who brought this mess to our attention in the first place, am I right?"

"Ah, yes, sir," Papalov answered, wishing he were someplace else. Worn to the bone from his five month ordeal and the hurried flight to DC, he could barely keep his eyes open.

"Stand up, man," Samuels ordered, agitated. "Please," he added, remembering the many times he had been chastised for his abusive manner.

"Yes, sir," Papalov said. Standing up too fast he knocked his chair backwards, but it was caught by a young woman before the high-back could hit the floor. With Darringer's help the chair was soon back where it belonged and Papalov, embarrassed, was facing the President again. He felt insignificant, nervous and downright stupid in front of so many high powered people. Why was the President singling him out? Was he going to jail? Or someplace worse?

"Would you mind telling the rest of us exactly what happened?" Samuels asked.

"I, we don't know, sir. I'm sorry. Nothing like this has ever happened before . . ."

"Damn it, Doctor, I know that! What do you *think* happened?"

Papalov shrugged. "The meteors went around Jupiter. They landed in all the seas of the Earth with the exception of the Arctic oceans. Not one speck of land was hit. They were, they had to be, guided by someone, or something. We haven't a clue. Our best guess, as bizarre as it may seem, is that we've been invaded by, well, we don't know."

"Jesus," Samuels said. He ran a hand through rough, bushy, black hair. "Jesus H. Christ, Doctor. What kind of an invasion are you talking about? I don't see any little green men running about, do you?"

"No, sir. Not yet, at any rate. The meteors all landed in relatively deep water. I, we, think, that if you examine the oceans, you'll find the answers there. Way down deep. Or maybe not so deep," Darringer added, hedging his bets.

Papalov searched the room, hoping for support from someone, anyone, but came away empty. Others looked at him as if he were a curiosity, perhaps mad, but no one spoke. Despite an air conditioned room Papalov began to sweat. They weren't blaming all this on him, were they? They came, they fell into the oceans, they disappeared. It was as simple as that. What did they want from him?

"We've already begun searching the oceans, Doctor," the Navy Chief of Staff, Roland Peronski, said, standing up and coming to Papalov's rescue. The admiral, a trim, fit, no-nonsense man of forty-five, looked to Samuels. "May I, Mr. President?" he asked.

"Please do, Admiral," Samuels said, nodding his way. Papalov, feeling relieved that somebody had volunteered for the hot seat, sat back down, almost knocking his chair over again.

Peronski returned the President's nod, then looked confidently around the room. A veteran of many campaigns, he had the respect of all those that knew him, and even those that didn't. He spoke, his deep voice reverberating about the room.

"To date, I'm sorry to say, we have found absolutely nothing, but it's only fair to say we've just begun. None of our ships were at sea when the storm hit, for obvious reasons, so all we've been able to deploy to date are the smaller vessels. They haven't ventured too far from shore yet, but we do have some data. We've discovered a marked increase in the temperature of the affected bodies of water, which was to be expected. This may, or may not, cause continued coastal flooding around the world. We'll have to wait and see if there's significant polar ice melt or not. We've managed some mineral samples from the Atlantic. The only change that we can see is a marked increase in the calcium content, and a slight increase in other minerals, phosphorus, potash and nitrogen to name a few. It appears, at this point in time, however, that the bodies were mostly composed of calcium carbonate. It's my understanding that, mixed with certain other chemicals, calcium is hard to ignite. The chemical also dissolves readily in water, which may explain why we haven't been able to locate any of them. They've apparently dissolved into our oceans."

"I thought meteors and such were composed of rocks and ice, heavy metals, things like that," the President commented. Trying to overcome a bad case of nerves, brought on by five months of pure hell, Samuels began to pace back and forth again. "Am I wrong?"

"We all thought that," an astronomy professor associated with MIT said, standing up. Unfamiliar with White House protocol, and nervous himself, he forgot to ask permission. "Until now, anyway. I think what the admiral is saying just proves how little we, as humans, know about our universe. Who could have forecast water on the moon? The many satellites of Jupiter, all different in composition and appearance? Every one. Now we apparently have meteors made of calcium, which is not that far out if you think about it. The white cliffs of Dover are composed of calcium. Perhaps our invaders originated on a planet made entirely of chalk? And who's to say we won't find a moon made of green cheese somewhere?"

Everyone laughed at the professor's remark. Everyone relaxed a bit. It had been a long, five-month nightmare. Everyone breathed easier. Except Papalov Darringer, who stood up, his fear of where he was dissipating, angry at the brevity.

"Listen," he said, looking around the room. "I hate to be the bad guy, but we're all forgetting three very important things here. First, those meteors were *guided* around Jupiter. They had to be. Second, they began slowing down three days out from Earth. This at a time when they should have been increasing their speed. And the third thing, the thing I find impossible to explain, is that not one of these things hit land. They didn't even strike within a mile of land. How do we explain that?"

Samuels stopped pacing. "What are you saying?" he asked. The room quieted down and all eyes focused on Papalov. His glasses slipped down his nose. He pushed them back up.

"That these meteors were guided by an alien form of intelligence. I don't know how, or why, but it's the only explanation. I hate to say it, Mr. President, but I think our troubles are just beginning."

Chapter 10
Troubled Waters

It wasn't until four months later, on a balmy, warm Wednesday in mid July, that Marsha was able to rent her house in Santa Monica. She and Jacob had decided to move south, into Jacob's house in San Diego. Married eight months now and still deeply in love, they rearranged furniture and set up house together. Things were picking up, the world had regained a semblance of order, and life was approaching good again.

Once the upstairs and main floor had been reshuffled and refurbished to Marsha's satisfaction, they went to work cleaning up Jacob's junky old basement. Two rooms were emptied, one of which contained all of Jacob's survival equipment, and condensed into one more organized room. Marsha heartily agreed with the idea of hoarding supplies, especially after the harrowing experience they had just gone through.

When that was done they discussed plans to expand the upstairs into three smaller rooms; a guest room and two offices, one each for Marsha and Jacob. First, however, since all their money was gone, Marsha would need to find a job, or find a publisher for her new book: "Pyramids, Dragons and Extraterrestrials: The Final Connection." It wasn't that her agent couldn't find a publisher, right now she was waiting for a final bid from four of them. Then there would be enough money to remodel and rebuild.

Like everyone else the Malfuscos had squandered what money they'd had in the months before the meteor's impacted. Like the rest of the world they were just getting on their feet again. They were in no hurry to get rich, however, as the newly married couple, now that the stress of impending doom had been removed from their marriage, found themselves enjoying each other more and more as time moved along. Anyway, they would have wealth enough as soon as Jacob received his advance for *his* new book: "Dragons are for Real" coming out in November. Jacob was to receive a healthy $150,000 for starters, and his book was already in demand, with a waiting line a mile long. He and Marsha were hoping they might retire from teaching and take up research and writing for a living. It had been a lifelong dream for both of them.

It wasn't until the movers came with Marsha's old piano that Jacob realized she actually played the thing.

"Not for a while," she said, directing the two beefy men towards the living room. "Not since I met you, anyway. It's a family heirloom. I had it put in for refinishing shortly before we met. And then we found out about the meteors. Didn't much feel like playing after that, so I just left it in the shop."

That evening after dinner, with a soft breeze pushing through the windows and the smell of honeysuckle heavy on the air, Jacob went down to the basement and retrieved his trombone from a corner room. After an hour of cleaning and polishing the instrument he presented it to Marsha.

"You're kidding me, right?" she said, her face lighting up. "You play trombone?"

"Not for a long time, Marsha. I can't remember when I last played the thing."

That evening, after several false starts, Jacob and Marsha got their rhythm and bearings and played together for the first time. Neighbors up and down the street, perturbed when the Malfuscos began tuning up, soon opened their doors and gathered in the streets to better listen in. Passersby on the sidewalks outside stopped and did the same. Marsha had been groomed to play concert piano when she was young, and Jacob had played for both his high school and college bands. As accomplished musicians do whenever they come together, the couple quickly caught onto the other's style and from then on it was easy. Overjoyed with one another, they played on into the night, classical, pop, rock and jazz, anything and everything, completely oblivious to the crowd gathered outside. The neighborhood moaned when the Malfuscos called it quits around eleven. Tired and ready for bed, Jacob and Marsha were both surprised, and pleased, when they heard the whistles and applause from their neighbors. They were not surprised when, in the early hours of the morning, their lovemaking took on new energy. Luckily they remembered to close the windows, otherwise they might have received another round of well deserved whistles and applause.

Marsha, among her other attributes, was a great cook. It hadn't been easy losing the weight they had lost as Marsha had a knack of endowing even the simplest of meals with extra calories. The morning after they had made such beautiful music together Marsha, in good appetite, cooked up a hearty Spanish omelet, adding cantaloupe, fresh strawberries and sliced oranges on the side, items recently introduced back into the market place. Both had some of Jacob's hoarded coffee to drink, minus the usual cream and sugar they both still craved.

"Something the matter?" Marsha asked as they both sat down to breakfast in the small dining room. All about them Jacob's plants, and a few of Marsha's, paraded their stuff. Those that had survived the onslaught, anyway. Much to his sorrow Jacob had lost the majority of the ones he'd had, having left them behind in wake of the world's impending doom. Now only the dining room and kitchen supported any living greenery. The local nurseries were doing their best to meet the demand, but it took a long time to grow a plant, and it was going to take even longer for the industry to get back on its feet. Like every commodity in the world, demand far outstripped supply, and the manufactories of the world wondered if they would ever catch up.

For the most part, Jacob was a happy man. Now that he only smoked outdoors, having not yet quit again, and Marsha had scrubbed both floor and walls until her hands and knees were raw, the house smelled as fresh and clean as a high mountain forest after a spring rain.

Jacob frowned and sat down, the morning's paper in his hands.

"According to the *Tribune* the world's fishing industries are having a tough time," he said, sipping at his coffee. "Fact is, fishing around the world is about wiped out. Catches are down two-thirds from this time last year. Crabbing, too. And it's getting worse."

"Does the paper say what's causing it?"

"Nobody knows for sure. Some of the scientists are saying it may have something to do with the increased calcium in the oceans. Others are saying the meteors impacting may have killed off most of the phyto and zoo plankton, destroying the food chain. That makes more sense than the calcium theory. What are the latest estimates? That five or six million of the damn things hit, and not the original two or three million?"

"Something like that," Marsha said, not that interested.

"Anyway, they don't have any answers. It's not good, at any rate. The world depends a great deal on the oceans for food, you know."

"Jacob Malfusco, I know! I'm a scientist too, remember? Quit patronizing me. Eat your omelet, it's getting cold."

"Sorry," Jacob said, forking a strawberry. "The upshot is," he said, taking a bite, "the Trib says we could be in for another world crisis. Hunger, in this case. It's already started."

"Jesus," Marsha said, putting down her fork. Jacob looked at his wife. Except for the first time they'd met she had never swore in front of him, and he couldn't honestly remember if she'd done it that time.

"If it's not one damn thing, it's another," Marsha muttered, looking out the window. She shook her head, wiped her mouth, and, trying to ignore what Jacob had just told her, went back to eating her omelet.

* * *

The following month a pod of killer whales were found dead, floating belly up in waters close to Alaska. What was left of them, anyway. They had been chewed to pieces. Soon to follow were sharks, seals, dolphins and other whales, all top predators of the oceans.

"Something mangled them," Jacob said over dinner. "Apparently the smaller fishes have turned to attacking the larger ones. In packs, or schools, or whatever. Like wolves, and lions, and piranha. Unheard of, but they're probably starving. It looks like their hunger is overcoming their fear."

"I read that," Marsha said, pouring vinegar on her tossed green salad. "Fishing nets are coming up empty, or with large holes torn in them. Weird. But I guess fish have always had teeth. Even the smaller ones."

"Yeah. I guess starving to death can change your mind about a lot about things. Speaking of which, ABC says most of the third world countries are beginning to starve, even worse than before. Mostly countries that depend heavily on fishing. The U.N. has predicted a worldwide famine in another couple of months unless something is done. They've also declared a moratorium on fishing, to try and find the cause and to give the oceans time to regenerate, but nobody's paying attention. Things are getting to be a real mess. Seems the marine biologists haven't a clue as to what's going on, or anybody else for that matter."

"Either that, or they do and are not telling us."

"Now there's a thought. But why? The funny part is, the plankton are thriving! They've made a great comeback. It doesn't look like they were affected that much in the first place. Something's definitely out of kilter. Wars start and people kill each other when they get hungry, baby. It don't look good. It don't look good at all."

Chapter 11
Invasion

A full moon in September saw the first of them come ashore. They came by the thousands, along every accessible beach along every coastline around the world. As the world turned they left the waters that could no longer nourish them and made landfall shortly after sunset. There they rested, and waited.

First to wade ashore were those off the Pacific coast from South to Central America, then from there on up the seaboard, beach by beach, to British Columbia and southern Alaska. The next invasion came ashore along the beaches of the Marquesses and Hawaiian Islands, Tahiti, Palmyra and all the other islands sandwiched between longitudes 135° and 165°. Moving west they lumbered ashore on the Pacific islands of Midway, Samoa, Tonga, the Aleutians and those directly beyond and in between. Beasts in numbers the likes of which Earth had not seen for thousands of years. Huge and menacing, with blazing, yellow eyes and insatiable appetites. Next came Kamandorskie Island in the North Pacific, Wake, Tarawa New Caledonia and New Zealand in the south. Hours later half the beaches in Australia, most of those in Japan, and every island in between the two were being invaded.

Shortly thereafter the entire coast of east China was covered with the creatures, along with the islands of the East Indies, the rest of Australia, and all of South Asia clear into Bangladesh. No island was too small, no beach too big, no continent too long. There were fifteen million, five hundred thousand of them, and they were hungry.

The smaller islands of the world were the first to be overrun. Once the alien life form adjusted to living on land, once their gills had developed into lungs and their flippers into legs and clawed feet, they began to move inland, devouring humans, tigers, pigs, cats, cattle, horses, goats, bears, corn and wheat, rice, grass, beans and strawberries. Anything and everything edible, including each other if ground were not given. With proper nourishment wings on massive shoulders, above the forelegs, began to develop. Scaled bodies glowed an iridescent green, with shades of red, pink and orange running along their sides. Legs and bellies turned green-black, as did the long, tapered tail, except where it terminated in a whale-like flipper resembling tanned leather tightly strung. One hundred razor-sharp teeth and fangs adorned a strikingly crocodilian head, on top of which rested a long, thin, rearward tapered plate, resembling that of its cousin, the pterandon, only larger, mimicking the flipper with its dressing of taught, leather-like skin.

Once metamorphosed, the immature Dragons moved with the quickness of cats and the cunning of lions. They were voracious eaters, needing to consume prodigious amounts of meat and produce on a daily basis to sustain their rapid growth. Their metabolism was engineered in such a way that they would grow from a foot long, eel-like creature to a huge, full grown, highly maneuverable, formidable predator in less than eight months. Arriving on shore under cover of darkness they took the armies of the world by complete surprise. The invasion would prove a massacre from the start.

* * *

It was hot along the Southern California coast, even hotter inland. A scorching desert wind, known to the locals as a Santa Ana, was working its way over the Laguna Mountains and smothering the coastal towns and beaches beneath a blanket of sweltering heat. Record numbers of people were being driven to the beaches in hopes of cooling off. Jacob, back to giving two seminars a day and teaching several classes in between, was as hot, tired and irritable as the rest of the population living in an around San Diego. Maybe even more so.

Marsha had spent the morning working on her new book and the afternoon cleaning house. Fans droned away in the kitchen and living rooms, but they didn't help much. She could afford to hire a maid, always could, but Marsha was homegrown and preferred to do the cleaning herself. After a supper of salad and cold cuts, around eight, the Malfuscos decided to get out of their overheated house for a while and go down to the beach. Since they seldom needed it, like most San Diegans the couple had no air conditioning, and the triple digit temperatures were beginning to make them ill.

"Ever been to the Ocean Beach pier?" Jacob shouted from the living room after helping Marsha clear the table.

"No. What's down there?" Marsha yelled back from the kitchen. Drying her hands on a well used apron she walked into the living room and sat down next to Jacob, joining him in a cross-wind of hard working fans.

"Well, they have a pier to start with. There's kind of a little food bar at the end. We can get a beer or something. It should be cooler there, and romantic.

Full moon tonight, according to the paper."

"Strange things happen when there's a full moon, Jacob Malfunction."

"Oh yeah? Like what?"

"Women have been known to get wild, for one thing."

"Even in one hundred degree heat?"

"Especially in one hundred degree heat," Marsha said, running her hand through Jacob's hair. She twirled at several strands there, a mischievous look in her eyes.

"What do you say?" Jacob said, pulling Marsha's hand from his head.

"To what?"

"To going down to the pier!"

"All right! God knows we could use a little romance around here lately."

* * *

Jacob was surprised to see the parking lot so full at nine in the evening, but then it was tourist season, and still warm out. Any cooling ocean breezes were being pushed back out to sea by the Santa Ana. Still, it was a good ten degrees cooler than Mission Hills, and the Malfuscos were glad they had come. Jacob parked his new BMW close to the water and got out. Radiance from a host of soft, yellow lights along the pier's guard rails danced off the surface of the boardwalk and the large breakers rolling beneath it.

Jacob stretched, took a deep breath and let it out before walking around to open the door for Marsha. Several campfires dotted the beach, further lighting a hazy, late evening sky. The air was filled with the pungent smells of burning wood and cooking food. Jacob loved the beach. He had practically grown up on it while in high school. And he had been a pretty fair surfer in his day. But that was long ago, before the rigors of college and a budding teaching career had set in.

"Wow!" Marsha exclaimed. "It's beautiful here! Kind of like Santa Monica, in a way." She took in her own, deep breath, held it, expelled slowly. "Why haven't you brought me here before?"

"Well, we haven't had a lot of time since we moved back, you know," Jacob answered, pleased that Marsha was pleased. They hadn't done much of anything since the scare except work. Everyone had had to work, and work hard, to bring the world back up to pre-swarm levels, and they still weren't there. Global hunger and famine were still prevalent in the poor countries, and many factories and farms were still down. Getting the world back in order was proving to be a slow, painful process. "Now that things are getting back to normal we'll come more often. I promise. I wouldn't mind learning to surf again, now that I've lost all that weight. Maybe I could teach you."

"Sounds good to me," Marsha said, though she had no desire whatsoever to learn the sport. "Now, where's that little bar?"

They walked, arm in arm, the short distance to the pier, then out onto it. Marsha took Jacob's hand and they walked quietly along, caught up in the moment, glad to be out of the house and away from all their work and the troubles of the world. The roar of crashing waves, along with the subdued radiance from the lights, did indeed make for a romantic evening. Halfway down the boarded walkway the Malfuscos stopped to talk to a fisherman and his two young sons. The tall, thin man wore cut off Levi's, a T-shirt, straw hat and sandals, same as his two boys. Jacob guessed them to be from one of the inland ranches.

"You guys catch anything?" Jacob asked. He bent over the railing and gazed into the water below. It was good to see the ocean blue-green again, and the sky black against the full moon and a hundred-thousand twinkling stars. The golden-yellow stuff had cast a wicked spell, he admitted, but Jacob, and everyone he knew, was long ago thankful the sky over San Diego had returned to its normal color. Still leaning over the rail Jacob heard a loud splashing off in the distance, followed by sounds of something tearing something else apart.

"You guys hear that?" Jacob asked, startled. He straightened up and looked around, half expecting something to jump out of the water at him.

"Hear what?" Marsha asked, gazing at the moon, lost in her own little, romantic world.

"Been splashin' like that all evenin'," the fisherman said. "Weird, 'specially since ain't supposed to be no fish around. Big ones, anyway. Lots a little fry swimmin' around, but no big ones. Not as far as I can tell, anyways."

"Got any ideas?" Jacob asked, stepping back from the rail.

"Could be sharks or dolphin," the man answered as his two boys leaned through the railing and peered around. "Might be some schools left. Saw some pretty big things, way out, earlier this evenin', before it got so dark. Saw their backs, anyway. I think it was their backs. Coulda been whales, maybe. Was hopin' I might catch one, just to see what they was."

Jacob looked at the children, fearful they might fall in, then back to the man. "I take it you haven't caught anything?"

"Nah," the man said. "There's not much doin' anymore. Not since the fish died out, or did whatever it was they did. But we still give it a try. Used to come here a lot. Still do. It's nice here, and it sure beats hell outta the inland heat!"

"I know what you mean," Jacob said. "Well, good luck," he added, then took Marsha's hand and the couple continued on their way. They hadn't gone another twenty feet when they heard the man scream. Jacob feared that one of the boys had fallen off the pier.

"Got one!" the man yelled, and Jacob felt immense relief. He and Marsha, along with several people close by, made an about face and hurried over. The man's fishing pole, a heavy-duty surfing rod, was bent over almost double. The farmer fought what ever he had for about half a minute. Sweat broke out on his face, and then his line snapped with a loud "TWANG" causing him to stumble backwards into the arms of a young couple who had been watching.

"Man, what was that?" he lamented once he had regained his balance. The farmer thanked the couple, then walked back to the rail and reeled in what was left of his line. "That was thirty pound test," he added with a frown, his children looking on and giggling. "Had to be pretty damn big to break that! Who said there was no fish left in the ocean?"

"What do you think it was?' Marsha asked.

"Coulda been a big halibut. Used to catch 'em here once in a while. More likely a shark, though. Damn! Pretty big, whatever it was."

"Maybe next time," Jacob smiled. He took Marsha's hand and made ready to leave.

"Thanks," the man said as the Malfuscos began making their way back down the pier. Others who had gathered around did the same, speculating among themselves as to what had happened.

"It's been a strange day," a fifteen-year-old boy, escorting his girl beside the Malfuscos, said. Marsha smiled at the couple, wondering if she had ever been that young.

"How's that?" Jacob asked, looking over at the boy.

"Some people drowned earlier. Got caught in a rip tide, or something. Found them down by the rocks. What was left of them, anyway. Got pretty beat up somewhere."

"Well, thanks for telling me," Jacob said, wondering why the kid was talking to him.

"Don't worry," the boy continued. "The lifeguards aren't letting anyone in the water. At least not too far out. Not tonight, anyway."

"What happens when the lifeguards leave?" Jacob asked. The boy and his girlfriend shrugged.

"That's comforting," Marsha interjected, looking around Jacob at the young couple.

The boy and girl smiled her way.

"Just thought you'd like to know," the boy said, then he and his girlfriend picked up their pace and moved off. "Stay out of the water!"

"Thanks," Jacob yelled after them as they departed.

"What time is it?" Marsha asked as the walked farther along the pier. She yawned and rested her head against Jacob's shoulder.

"Almost nine-thirty. Why? You ready to go home?"

"I just asked," Marsha said. "This night air is making me drowsy. And quit being so grumpy!"

A few more steps down the walkway and the screaming started. It wasn't the fisherman this time, but a chorus of voices coming from the beach, back where they had come from. Jacob and Marsha whirled in time to see shadows running off the sands and onto the parking lot. A door slammed and shots rang out as the Malfuscos hurried to the guard rail for a better look. One of the bullets hit a lamp post next to Jacob and caromed off, making a loud "whanging" sound. Jacob's heart skipped a beat.

"Get down!" he yelled, grabbing Marsha by the arm and pulling her to the boardwalk. Jacob crawled on top of her, trying to shield her from danger. More shots thudded into the planking around them. A high pitched screeching filled the air, drowning out the screams. Jacob clenched his teeth against the grating sound.

"What's going on?" Marsha asked, finding it hard to breathe with two hundred pounds on top of her. "You're squishing me. Get off!"

"Must be some kind of gang war! We need to get out of here."

"Fine!" Marsha said, trying to squirm free. "But first you have to get off me!"

Jacob rolled off, then got to his knees. He shielded his eyes from the overhead lights as he peered through the rails. Another shot was fired, followed by the revving of engines and the squealing of tires. Jacob heard the unmistakable crunch of cars and trucks backing into each other. There was yelling and shouting now, mixed with the screams, as if people along the beach were trying to get organized, trying to help each other. But against what?

Finally Jacob saw them. Huge shapes lumbering out of the water before stopping on the beach, only to move on again, pushing against one another and screeching. Jacob, his eyes adjusting to the dim light and the distance, saw several of them chewing on something, their massive jaws working back and forth. And then he saw the bodies. Human bodies, a dozen or so, in halves and quarters and pieces, lying up and down the beach. Jacob felt terror, and became sick to his stomach.

"Jesus," Jacob whispered, recognizing the shapes. "I don't believe this."

"Believe what?" Marsha said, feeling her husband's panic. She moved closer to Jacob, on her knees, and looked towards the beach. "What are you talking about? What do you see?"

Jacob got to his feet and crouched, pulling Marsha up with him. "I'll tell you later! Right now we've got to get out of here before those things start moving off the beach, before they block our exit. Everybody!" Jacob shouted, looking right and left. "Get off the pier. Now! It's our only chance!"

Taking Jacob's cue, close to a hundred people began running back up the pier. Panic set in as men, women and children began screaming and running over one another. The fisherman threw his pole into the water, scooped up his two boys and took off towards the exit. The Malfuscos were quick to follow, running as fast as their out-of-shape legs could carry them.

By the time they reached their car the parking lot was a mess. People continued to smash into each other's vehicles in their haste to get out. Horns honked as cursing and more screams filled the air. Fights broke out. Jacob fumbled with his keys, trying to get the right side door open. His heart was pounding so hard he thought it might give out. With some dismay he noticed the rear of his treasured BMW was crumpled.

"Damn it," he muttered, finally finding the right key. Over Marsha's protests he manhandled her into the car, slamming the door behind her. Running to his side he glanced towards the beach. The pier lights and the campfires were still illuminating the area, although it was harder to see now. Jacob stopped. He could make out the outlines of many bulky shapes up and down the beach. They seemed to be resting, spaced almost evenly apart from one another, like pigeons at roost, giving each other limited room. Yellow eyes blazed in the dark. Hungry, frightening eyes. Over by the jetty to his right he could make out several of the large shapes moving laboriously up the rocks. Several were resting on top, silhouetted against the moon and the lights of Mission Beach to the north. There seemed to be hundreds of them on the beach, crowded, jostling one another in places, just resting there, as if waiting for someone, or something, to guide them. Jacob shivered.

Jacob opened the door Marsha had unlocked for him. He felt creepy, out of place, as if the land he was standing on now belonged to someone else, and if he didn't get off he would pay the price. Over by the apartments and houses that lined the parking lot hundreds of people were milling about and looking towards the ocean. They moved slowly, children among them, in singles and bunches, jabbering and curious as to what was going on. Jacob waved and shouted for them to stay back, to get the hell out of there. Some of them stopped, but most moved cautiously forward, wanting to see what was going on, wanting to be in on the action.

"Damn fools," Jacob muttered, still standing outside the car. He looked in at Marsha. "Hand me my camera. It's in the glove compartment."

"You must be crazy!" Marsha said, fighting to keep her supper down. "Can't you see what's going on? Get in the God damn car!"

"They're not moving! Now give me the camera. I'll only be a second."

Reluctant, Marsha opened the glove compartment and handed Jacob his camera. Over Marsha's protests he began walking the short distant to the beach. Jacob turned and put his finger to his lips, asking Marsha to be quiet. The last of the cars shot out of the lot as neighbors continued to inch forward. A lone police car, lights flashing, swung into the parking area and slid to a stop far away from Jacob. Once Jacob had turned his back Marsha got out of the car, went around and sat in the driver's seat. With trembling hands she started the engine.

Jacob reached the edge of the lot and hid behind a clump of pygmy date palms. The creatures were still on the beach, barely moving. Some of them were still chewing on human remains, blood running out of their mouths. Others stared eastward, as if sizing up the situation. Jacob caught several pairs of yellow eyes gazing his way, but stood his ground. He took several quick shots, his camera lighting up the beach. When several of the beasts made a move in his direction, Jacob turned and ran. Once back at the car he was thankful Marsha had the car running. He leaned on the BMW's roof and motioned towards the crowd.

"Don't go down there!" he yelled between ragged breaths. "Go back where it's safe and call the police! Call the National Guard! Do anything, but don't go down there!"

People looked at him as if he was crazy. A few hesitated, but most continued on, moving faster now. Two more police cars, accompanied by an ambulance, swung into the lot but the crowd never hesitated. Kids and dogs ran ahead of the adults, braver now that the police had arrived. Jacob cursed, then got into the BMW. Marsha roared out of the lot, barely missing a young couple running towards the beach, laughing and having a great time. The Malfuscos took a last look back and headed for home, passing more police cars and several fire engines on the way. Jacob felt a little better, but he was not sure what a handful of men and women could do against hundreds of huge, vicious, juvenile Dragons.

* * *

Shortly afterwards, as the full moon was fast disappearing behind a high fog bank, dozens more of the beasts made their way through the jetty and onto the beaches of Mission Bay. Simultaneously hundreds of others were swimming past Point Loma towards the shores of San Diego Bay. There they struggled out of the water, looking for a place to rest, a place where their rapid metamorphosis from sea creatures to land dwellers could end its painful process. Anyone caught in the water, or near it, became a quick meal. Hysterical people, out to cool off and relax, out for an evening stroll, screamed and ran off into the fog, anywhere to get off the beach and reclaim their sanity.

In less than an hour the juvenile Dragons had established beachheads along the entire west coast of North America. Within twenty-four hours every island and every coastline of every continent had been invaded. Once on shore the alien invaders waited while gills fused and lungs and other body parts developed. Massive muscles lining the shoulders, originally used to control dorsal fins, now supported rapidly developing wings. All around the globe, at dawn's first light, their bodies now transformed from sea creatures to land dwellers, their complete metamorphosis lacking only at the wings, mankind's newest threat, hungry and out of sorts, began moving off the beaches, looking for their next meal.

A terrified world beat a hasty retreat. Resistance was mounted as quickly as possible. Tanks, airplanes and other vehicles of modern warfare were brought in where there had been enough warning. But it takes time to mobilize an army, and the world, for the most part, was caught completely flat footed. She was disorganized and inept for the first forty-eight hours of the invasion. By the time humanity realized what was happening the beasts had moved inland, into the cities and towns and surrounding countrysides. For all their size they were hard to see, possessed of chameleon like qualities, able to blend in with their surroundings, making them almost invisible when not on the move. Man had missed his chance to destroy the invaders when they had been most vulnerable, when they had rested, out in the open and almost defenseless, on the beaches of Earth.

Within a scant three days, the immature Dragons would almost double in size, their wings would be fully developed and they would become the airborne killers they were designed to be instead of land dwelling monsters. Already a formidable fighting machine, the invaders would soon become mankind's greatest nightmare.

Chapter 12
Denver, CO, 48 Hours Later

The President of the United States sipped at a glass of water and straightened up. Known to be humorous in difficult situations, this morning Jack Samuels was anything but. The large meeting room he had commandeered in one of Denver's finer hotels was packed. Every chair was full, standing room only. His cabinet members and key Congress personnel sat in front, followed by higher echelon military and science advisors, plus an assortment of other persons he deemed vital to his country's survival. Only the press was missing. The country was in such disarray there had been no time to invite them, and, in truth, he didn't want them there anyway. His country was in panic, and his people didn't need the press giving them false or misguided evidence, further terrifying them.

Samuels' gazed around the room, finding it hard to speak. Most of the people he knew, some he didn't. They had all been flown in shortly after the invasion, but this would be their first meeting together.

"All right," he said, clearing his throat. He set the glass of water back down on the podium and searched the room. "I'd like to thank you all for coming to Denver on such short notice. You all know why you're here. Our nation, indeed the world, is facing a crisis the likes of which mankind has never seen, nor dreamed of. Left with the residue of a starving planet after the meteors struck we were already in sad shape before this invasion started. As far as I know we're one of the few countries still on our feet, one of the few with a fighting chance. Now, that said, I'd like to start this meeting with a few hard questions. Is there a Professor Jacob Malfusco in the room?"

Jacob, startled by his name being called so soon, stepped forward from where he'd been standing next to a wall to the President's right. Marsha stood to his left and, by sheer coincidence, Papalov Darringer stood to his right. Neither of them had ever met.

"Here, sir," Jacob said, raising his hand, his stomach churning. Tired from the flight to Phoenix by Lear Jet and the ensuing hop to Denver, he and Marsha had slept little since the invasion began.

Samuels looked him over. He had never met Jacob, and only knew of him by way of one of his advisors. "I understand you're the man that discovered the Dragon skeleton?"

"Yes, sir," Jacob answered nervously. "That would be me."

"And I understand, on word from my advisors, that you think these things that have invaded our worlds are your so called Dragons, too? Of the same breed?"

"That would be my guess, ah, ah . . ."

Marsha gave Jacob an elbow, then whispered in his ear: "It's *Mr. President,* dummy."

". . . Mr. President," Jacob finished. Several people around the room laughed. Jacob reddened visibly.

"We're not here for guesses, Jacob," Samuels said. "We don't have the time."

"No, sir," Jacob said, gathering himself. "What I meant is, I'm fairly certain they're the same. At this point in time, anyway."

"Would you mind stepping up here with me and showing the rest of us how you came to this conclusion?"

Jacob reddened some more as he moved towards the front of the room. People moved out of his way, people he didn't know and had never seen. Jacob felt all the eyes in the room focused his way, the eyes of the most powerful men and women in the United States, not to mention the world.

Jacob made his way onto a large stage, behind the podium, where two movie screens had been set up by prior arrangement, Jacob having been forewarned. Samuels gestured for a Marine Corps sergeant at the rear of the room to dim the lights. Once they were down a young woman in the middle of the room activated two slide machines. People behind her, and around the room, jostled for a better view. The President moved to one side of the stage and leaned against the wall there.

After several misfires a picture of George appeared on the left screen, a side angle shot of his bare bones hanging from the museum roof in San Diego. A picture of several juvenile Dragons, from Jacob's personal photos at the beach, quickly filled the opposite screen, followed by gasps and exclamations from the crowd. People began talking among themselves, excited, nervous, skeptical talk until the President stepped in and stopped it. Once the crowd had calmed down he handed Jacob a pointer and went back to lean against the wall.

As nervous as he was Jacob went forward, confident in his knowledge and abilities. He pointed to the picture of the juvenile Dragons, resting beside one of the campfires on the beach, then looked out over his audience. For the first time he noted the preponderance of military men and women. Admirals and generals, captains and colonels, from all branches of the armed forces. There were a lot of suits, too, and Jacob wondered why everyone, except the President, was so dressed up when the world was falling apart.

"Ah," Jacob began, turning his back to the screens, "if you will please note the similarities here. The protrusions that are turning into wings at last report. The long, tapered tail with the whale-like flipper at the end, making this creature highly maneuverable in both water and air. The tails are multi-directional. By that I mean, unlike a whale, who can only move its tail up and down, George and his kin can move theirs in any direction, similar to your wrist and hand. Quite a feat as you can imagine. There's no other flying creature like this one on Earth, nor has there ever been to the best of my knowledge. But then we didn't know George existed until we found him, did we?"

Jacob paused for a moment to let the information sink in. Over towards the back Marsha, proud of her man, smiled and waved his way. Jacob returned the compliment, then continued.

"Notice also the large, backward curving plate on the head, just like George. This can also be used both in the air and the water. It's similar to pterandons—flying reptiles—that inhabited the Earth millions of years ago. Ladies and gentlemen, Mr. President, it's my conclusion that these creatures will be turning into flying machines more maneuverable, and deadly, than anything mankind has ever encountered, or thought of encountering. It's T-Rex with wings. And yes, they're somehow related to George. I don't see any way around that conclusion. But as to how, I haven't a clue."

Jacob paused and looked at the projectionist. "Do you mind turning to a picture of the reconstruct?" he asked, becoming more confident as the minutes ticked by. He was in his element now and nobody knew more about these things than he did. The young woman nodded and shortly an image of George—as a highly skilled artist had depicted him when alive—replaced the skeleton on the screen. Most of those present in the room gasped. Except for the lack of wings and their size, the juveniles on the beach appeared exactly like George.

"Ladies and gentlemen," Jacob said, turning from the screen to face his audience, "I'm afraid, as all of you have no doubt figured out by now, that our world has been invaded by Dragons, or creatures we've always thought of as Dragons. More fierce and predatory than our wildest imaginations, and more dangerous than all the creatures depicted in all the drawings and literature passed down to us throughout our brief history as intelligent beings."

The room, buzzing but seconds before, fell into an ominous silence. People sat stunned and disbelieving, digesting the news in their individual ways. Another minute passed before the President found courage to walk towards center stage and have the lights turned back on. Then he gave everyone the go ahead for questions and stood to the right of Jacob, his arms crossed, as if to lend him support should the need arise.

"What you're saying is that these things are the Dragons of legend?" Jeremy Baldwin, the Secretary of Commerce, asked. A tall, lean, distinguished looking black man in his early fifties, Jeremy sat in the front row.

"Yes, sir," Jacob answered. "I believe so. I've done a lot of thinking since the Dragons came ashore. I've come to the conclusion, as my wife has, that our Earth has been invaded before. Perhaps many times. I believe they are the reason for a lot of our so-called sudden die outs our planet has suffered over the millennia. The woolly mammoths, nine-ten thousand years ago. Neanderthal man, thirty-six thousand years ago. A lot of unexplained disappearances over the years. The famines, diseases. Their appearance can answer a lot of old questions, and ask a lot of new ones."

General Alex Jackson, Marine Crops Commandant, decided he'd heard enough. A wiry, diminutive, battle hardened veteran of many campaigns, he didn't believe in fairy tales.

"You can't be serious," he said, standing up in the third row. The general stood on his toes and leaned on the chair in front of him to be better seen and heard. "You think these things have been invading our planet for thousands of years? That's about as stupid a thing as I've heard. Whatever for?"

"Food, General. Food from our oceans, food from our land. We're a planet that produces a lot of food, biomass if you will. Always has, always will. Unless we screw it up. Continue to screw it up, I mean. I think George is a relic. I believe he got left behind when the others departed. I believe all the Dragons, serpents and worms from our mythology were relics, too. Relics from a previous invasion, the last occurring around nine thousand years ago, at the dawn of human civilization. Why else do we find Dragon similarities all around the world? At a time when there was little contact among differing human tribes? Artifacts are all over the place. In the Mideast, Central America, Europe, India, the Orient. Everywhere."

"Are they intelligent?" a woman yelled from the back of the room, ignoring the fact that General Jackson had the floor. The general waited with the rest of the room for Jacob's answer.

"God, let's hope not!" Jacob yelled above increasing chatter. "In any case, it's too soon to tell. Right now they're still juveniles. They may gain in intelligence as they grow. I don't see why not, all living vertebrates do. How smart they'll get is anybody's guess. Right now we have little or no information on their intelligence. Sorry."

"They were inside the meteors, then?" Admiral Roland Peronski asked, standing up from where he'd been sitting next to General Jackson. The admiral's large, beefy frame contrasted sharply with the smaller general's. "They came down in the damn things, didn't they?"

"It looks that way," Jacob said. "The meteors were egg shells of a sort. They dissolved shortly upon entering the oceans and released their larvae, or Dragon fry, or whatever you want to call them. The larvae ate the smaller fishes, grew, and then ate the large ones. It may take centuries, or longer, for our seas to recover. Now they're on land, doing the same thing. By the way it's going they'll be full grown before we know it."

"Then what happens?" the admiral asked.

"You're guess is as good as mine, Admiral. Sorry."

Jacob pointed to a middle aged, Hispanic woman towards the middle of the room for his next question.

"Professor, these things are so huge. How can they possibly fly?" she asked.

"Their bones are hollow, for one thing," Jacob answered as the two military men sat back down. "Like a bird's. The leather membrane covering parts of the body is sandwich bag thin, yet tough as nails. Even at that, physics tells us they're still too heavy to fly. We believe these things originated on a heavier planet than Earth. A good analogy would be our people on the moon. They kind of float around up there. Here, on Earth, we figure the Dragons will kind of float around. Or will, once they get their wings."

"But, technically, they were born *here*, on our world."

"Right you are. Until we have children born on the moon I don't think anybody can guess the answer to your question correctly. Let's just say, at this point in time, I don't think these creatures are going to have any trouble flying in our atmosphere. Fact is, I think they're going to teach us a thing or two before . . . before this is all over with. They'll be strong, and fast, and highly maneuverable. I'm not a military man, but, from what I know, I don't think we'll have anything in the air that can bring them down, short of a head-on collision. Pardon my French, ladies and gentle, but I think we're going to be up against one mean mother-fucker."

Jacob paused, but no one spoke or raised a hand. He could feel the despair spreading about the room, the hopelessness. Feelings that had been growing since the beasts had first come ashore.

"I'm sorry," he said. "But the President called me here because of my expertise, and I think you all should know what we're up against."

"You won't mind if some of us disagree, will you?" an angry Walter Taffey, Air Force Chief of Staff, asked from his seat next to Admiral Peronski. The gray-haired general didn't bother to stand up. With half a right leg missing from a late night mission during the Muslim Wars he would rather sit. Taffey was upset. "Personally, I don't care what or who it is my boys are up against, Mr. Malfusco, we can take them out. Especially some God damn flying lizard! Stick to what you know, Professor. Me and my boys will take care of the rest."

"I hope you're right, General," Jacob said, scrutinized the balding, heavy set man. "But have you ever tried to shoot a bird out of the sky? A dove, for instance, that can climb and dive or change directions on a whim? No airplane can do that, not even our most sophisticated helicopters. I'm sorry, I think you're going to find we're on a totally different chess board here."

Taffey's response was to fold his arms and sit straighter. Aaron Cable, the President's military Chief of Staff, was next to speak. Not bothering to raise his hand the tall, thin, mustachioed rail of a man just stood up and spoke, as he had been used to doing all his life.

"Tell me, Professor," he began, and his manner was arrogant and blustering, "tell me if these Dragons of yours breathe fire too, will you? Do we have any chance at all?"

Jacob kept calm as a ripple of laughter spread throughout the room. He had expected it sooner or later. All he could do was try and make them believe him. "Not that we know of," he said.

"Well, at least there's that. I guess we can at least leave the water cannons in mothballs," Cable said to more laughter.

Jacob looked the general in the eye. "They're still immature, General," he said evenly. "Fire may come later. You people can joke all you want about this, but if you saw the mangled bodies of the people at Ocean Beach I don't think you'd be laughing. All the Dragons from our history breathed fire, so I don't see why these won't. Maybe those of you that think this is funny, maybe we should put *you* in the front lines, *without* a water hose."

The President, not wanting to anger his generals further, moved closer to

Jacob and put his hand on his shoulder.

"Mr. Malfusco is right," Samuels said, leaning into the mike. "I can guarantee any of you, who have never seen one of these things, that they are nothing to sneer about. They chased us out of the White House in less than twenty-four hours. I want you all to get serious here, or I *will* have you in the front lines. These creatures will not be taken lightly. Now, or ever. Now, are there any more questions for the professor?"

Unhappy, the general sat back down, a scowl on his face. He had never lost a battle in his life, and was not about to start now. Jacob answered a few more questions, then took his place towards the back of the room with Marsha.

"You did good!" Marsha whispered into his ear. Much to Jacob's embarrassment she put her arms around his waist and squeezed. Jacob squeezed back and smiled at the people looking his way. Up on the stage the President stood behind the podium.

"Ladies and gentlemen," he began, his face lined with worry, "as of this moment I am declaring a national emergency, a state of war. I'll ask my cabinet and military advisors to stay. The rest of you are excused for now, and I apologize for the short meeting. I hope you will understand. We need to get going here. After I've met with my staff I'll make an announcement to the public. A state of martial law is now in effect. Several other countries have done the same, and I expect the rest to follow in due course. I've been in contact with other heads of state and we've all agreed to help one another in this matter. As much as we can, anyway. Now, if the rest of you will step outside, I need to talk to my people here."

* * *

After the others had left and guards had been stationed beside the doors, Samuels gathered his staff together in a small conference room adjacent to the meeting room. There was coffee and hot water for tea on a large oak table, plus doughnuts and rolls, but no one was hungry.

"Alex," Samuels said, once everyone had been seated, "how do we stand from where you sit? No pun intended."

"We're deploying now, sir," the Marine Corps Commandant answered. "All leaves and days off have been canceled. We've got tanks and armored vehicles armed and ready to roll. Most of our pilots are in the air, and have been for some time. We're recalling all our units from overseas, as ordered. We're ready when you are, Mr. President."

"Aaron?" Samuels asked his Joint Chief's Chairman.

"We're about where the Marines are, Jack. Orders have been issued to mobilize all National Guard units. We should be fully operational in a day or two."

"That's the best you can do?" Samuels said, trying to hide his anger. "A day or two? People are dying in droves out there, General. How can I issue orders if you're not ready?"

Cable shuffled in his seat. He'd seen a lot of president's come and go, and he wasn't about to be intimidated by this one. "It takes awhile, Jack. We weren't forewarned, you know. Considering we've got about three hundred thousand more troops to assemble than the Corps I think we're doing all right. All of our bases along the coast were pretty much overrun before my men could even get out of bed, if you will remember. And another thing. These creatures are already in the back streets of our coastal cities. Not only do they blend in with their surroundings and are almost impossible to see, but we can't use heavy weapons with our own people running around, can we? I mean, kill our own women and children and all?"

"No, I guess we can't," Samuels said wearily. He poured himself a cup of coffee, offered the decanter to anyone else who wanted it. "Wanda," he asked of his Secretary of the Interior, "how are the evacuations coming? You said they've already started?"

"Not good, Mr. President, I'm sorry to say," Ms. Grayfeather answered. Usually prim and proper, the forty-nine-year-old American Indian woman was in a state of disarray this morning. "Like the general said, this has all happened too fast. Our coastal cities are in chaos, the bigger the city the worse things seem to be. There's mass panic and people are stampeding each other in an effort to get out. If they try to hide in their homes the Dragons are too strong. They virtually destroy stick houses. Mobiles are no defense at all. The only places that might be safe are the larger concrete buildings, but you can't cram everyone into those. And even if you could, with no water or food how long will they last? There's no place to hide, and nowhere to run. Those out in the country are safe for the time being. Right now we're in the process of trying to arrange for their evacuation. We're coordinating with the military in setting up refugee camps outside the larger inland cities. I don't know how effective they'll be, however, once Mr. Malfusco's Dragons begin to fly."

Jack Samuels frowned. After a few seconds his eyebrows furrowed and he took on the determined look that had helped him win the presidency.

"Well," he said, "then I guess it's up to us to see that they never get off the ground, isn't it?"

His people seated around the table looked at each other and wondered just how in hell they were going to do that.

Chapter 13
Oppama, Japan

Myoko Tanaguchi, age eleven and a beautiful child by anyone's standards, ran from her house and into the dense forest behind it. She had waited long enough. Her mother, father and older brother had gone to work that morning and never come home. The sun was setting behind the western hills and they had always come home before sunset. Myoko was frightened. There had been shooting along the coast all day long. Japanese airplanes had been flying over the city since early that morning, dive bombing and firing bullets at she knew not what.

Myoko climbed a small hill and looked down on her city by the sea. Most of it was in flames, and smoke billowed inland, to the south of her. Another earthquake had been the first thing to enter her mind. Like the one she had experienced at age seven, only worse. Several policemen and soldiers had run up her street this morning, bearing arms. Japanese soldiers and police never carried firearms in public, at least not that she'd ever seen. The young girl shivered. If this was not an earthquake, what was it? Were they at war? Were there riots in the city? There were so many questions, and no one to answer them.

Myoko sat down and leaned against a tree, fighting back tears. Overhead a trio of military jets roared by, the noise from their afterburners flooding the forest. After a while, after the jets were long gone, Myoko removed her hands from her ears and opened her eyes. Now the silence, and not the noise, was unnerving. Finding little comfort in the woods, Myoko rose to her feet and started back home. She had walked but a short distance when she heard the sound of heavy, labored breathing off to her right. There was a rancid stench in the air, a smell she'd never experienced before. Forgetting her fear and worried that someone had been shot, Myoko tiptoed towards the sound. It wasn't long before she found the injured Dragon lying on its side in some heavy undergrowth. There were wounds to both front legs and another to its side. Red blood flowed freely to the ground. The creature, its covering of scales and skin the mint green color of the forest, gazed at Myoko with big, inquisitive eyes. It snorted, and Myoko jumped.

After several minutes of hiding behind a tree, Myoko found renewed courage and stepped out into the open. Her fear dissipating, Myoko looked the Dragon over. She had heard about Dragons, read about them, but was not aware that any lived in her forest. No one had told her. Some were good and some were bad, according to legend. Since this one was not attacking or breathing fire it must be a good one. She would make it her pet! Myoko had heard that, once tamed, Dragons made good pets. Her friend at school had told her so. But first she needed to tend its wounds and feed it. Something so big must be hungry all the time. Myoko ran out of the woods towards her house, all her worries and fears forgotten. Her very own Dragon. She would be the envy of all her friends!

Myoko retrieved towels, blankets and medications from the bathroom, followed by food and water from the kitchen. All she could carry, in buckets and bags. She gathered leftover udon and sashimi, added some tofu and grabbed a half gallon of milk to go along. Dragons loved milk. It said so in all the books.

"I shall name him Fujisan, after our mountain," she exclaimed as she ran from the house, overloaded with all the supplies she had gathered.

Myoko hurried back and offered the Dragon what she had. Fujisan flinched when Myoko began cleaning her wounds, but somehow knew the young female was trying to help. When the cleaning was done, the wounds patched and the food was gone the Dragon, breathing heavily, lay back and tried to rest. Myoko scrutinized Fujisan from a distance. The beast had been watching her as her dog used to; with big, sad, loving eyes. She was startled when Fujisan began wagging the tip of its tail. The huge creature watched her for a while, wagging away, then closed its eyes and slept.

"I must go now," Myoko said after a while, after the sun had set and the night air began taking on a chill. She waited for some response from her friend, but, when none was forthcoming, she picked up her buckets and headed towards home. Down below the fires were still raging as bad as they had that morning. Shots were still being fired and Myoko thought she heard screaming from time to time. She waited well into the evening for her family to come home but, when they failed to show, when the sun had vanished and the skies became filled with smoke and ash and eerie screeching, when darkness overtook her home and the lights would not work, Myoko became frightened again. She made her way back through the forest, flashlight in hand and blankets in tow. There, on a bed of boughs and pine needles, she snuggled against Fujisan. Together they slept the night through, newfound friends in a hostile world.

Chapter 14
Colorado Springs, Colorado

Jacob gazed out the hotel window towards Pike's Peak. He and Marsha had been given the room free of charge, courtesy of the United States Government. They were billeted, along with a host of other scientists and advisors, in one of Colorado Springs better hotels. About twenty minutes away was Cheyenne Mountain Air Force Base, the hollowed out mountain that housed NORAD, America's main defense headquarters. Jack Samuels had set up his operations camp there and had invited Jacob, foremost Dragon expert in the world, to join him. Marsha was allowed to tag along, a fact that didn't set at all well with her.

"How come they listen to you and they don't listen to me?" she asked, sitting across from Jacob on the king sized bed.

"I don't know, honeypot. *I* listen to you."

"And don't call me honeypot! You know I don't like that."

"Sorry."

"I don't like it here!" Marsha continued, on a note she'd been sounding since arriving in Colorado Springs. She got off the bed and stood up. "This dinky little room. No stove, that crummy little ice box. How relaxing is this? I want to go home, Jake. I don't want to spend my last days like this, holed up in some crummy hotel room."

"It's not crummy, and there is no home. You know that," Jacob said. He stared at the peak with its new crop of snow, wondering if there were any Dragons up there. People hurried by on the streets below. Cars honked. Colorado Springs was busting at the seams. Military vehicles rumbled up and down the streets. Soldiers frequented the many shops, bars and restaurants. It was more like a military base now than a tourist town. Still, it was peaceful compared to the rest of the world. Jacob found it hard to believe that people and animals were being slaughtered by the millions only a thousand miles from his doorstep.

"San Diego's gone," Jacob said, turning from the window to face Marsha. "Los Angeles, San Francisco, Portland and Seattle on the west coast. Everything in between. New York, DC, Miami, Charleston and the whole eastern seaboard. There's been nothing from the Hawaiian Islands for twenty-four hours now. Japan's been overrun. Africa's a disaster. So is India. Only the countries with halfway decent armies are surviving. At least here the food's free, there's plenty of it, and we're alive."

"So far," Marsha said, facing Jacob. "What's going to happen when those things start flying all over the place? What then? People are already starving, and it's only been three days! What happens when all the food is gone?"

Marsha stopped and slumped back down on the bed. Tears came to her eyes. Jacob handed her his handkerchief and watched while she wiped at her eyes and blew her nose. "I'm sorry," she said, looking up at him. Her hands trembled. "If I have to die, then I want to do it at home, Jake. Not here, in some strange place with strange people."

"Nobody said anything about dying!" Jacob said, exasperated over his wife's attitude of late. Frustrated, he sat down beside her and rubbed her back. "Look, we'll be home before you know it. I promise. Right now Colorado Springs is the safest place to be. You know that, and I'm sure the military has everything under control by now. At least here in the United States."

* * *

Jack Samuels rolled out of his black limo and half-walked, half-ran to his new headquarters. A moderate wind swept down out of the Rockies to the west, bringing with it cold, brisk air. Off to the east a huge, red-brown sun was rising over the plains, casting an eerie gloom over the military base.

"I thought sunrises out here were supposed to be orange, or gold or something," Samuels said to his Secretary of Defense, Harold Adams. Short and stocky, Adams hurried to keep up, his legs no match for the president's longer ones.

"It's brown from the fires, Jack," Adams said. "All the fires to the east of us. There must be hundreds of them by now. The only thing saving our asses are the early rains."

Samuels bowed his head and picked up his pace, more to get out of the wind than anything. The military base brought back old memories of his years spent as an Air Force pilot and the part he had played, as a young man, in the Muslim Wars. A big part, as it had turned out. But he was older now, and tired. Bone tired. He hadn't slept in three days, or was it four? It was hard to sleep when the world you lived in was falling apart.

Once inside The Mountain the President grabbed a doughnut and a cup of coffee from the coffee bar and then hurried towards his designated conference room. It was cold inside, and Samuels pulled his coat a little tighter, accidentally leaving some chocolate doughnut smeared here and there. Once inside the room he made his way to the head of a long, wide, highly-polished oak table. There his subordinates stood and saluted or nodded his way, depending on their position. Overhead long rows of fluorescent lights flooded the chamber. Despite its brightness Samuels disliked the room and The Mountain it was housed in. He felt like a holed up coward, already defeated. The President noted his cabinet and military officers were as tired and worn as he was. He doubted many of them had slept either. Samuels waved everyone back into their seats.

"General Cable, I hope you have some good news for us this morning," Samuels said, continuing to stand. He eyed his military commander and braced himself for some kind of arrogant answer, but Cable avoided his eyes.

"I'm afraid I have none," the general answered, reworking a pile of papers on the table in front of him. Finding his courage he looked at Samuels. "The Dragons are beginning to move out of the coastal cities and towns and into the countryside," he began, tapping his fingers on the table while he spoke. "Everything along both coasts has been torn apart. Totally in ruins. We believe that close to two-thirds of the people living in them are dead. Maybe more. Those that are left are holed up like terrified rabbits. Fires are out of control. Our fire fighters and police are afraid to get out into the open, and justifiably so. It's a mess, Mr. President. Our counterattacks have been futile for the most part. I've not allowed rockets or heavy artillery to be used in the cities, let alone tanks and the like. Too many civilians. Your specific orders, sir."

"I remember, Aaron. Thank you. General Jackson, how about you? Anything decent to report?" the President asked, turning to face his Marine Corps Commandant.

"I'm afraid not, Mr. President. Malfusco's Dragons are proving to be quick, and smart. They hear our tanks coming and they retreat. They don't go head to head, like a normal enemy. Guerrillas, down to the last one. They hide. They blend into their surroundings. They're elusive and, unfortunately, small arms fire and rifles don't seem to bother them. We're going to need heavier weapons, sir."

The President sighed. "What else, Alex?"

"Like Aaron said, they're moving out into the country. My men are starting to make some headway there, without people all around. Our tanks and light artillery are doing some good, but . . ."

"But what?" Samuel's asked.

"To be honest, Mr. President, we can't keep up with them. One minute they're there, the next they're not. Our men, and armor, are too slow. Sorry, sir. This is proving tougher than we had imagined. If only our armored divisions were faster, we'd have a better chance."

"If ifs and buts were candy and nuts what a sweet world this would be, General."

"Yes, sir."

"Walter?" Samuels said, looking towards his General of the Air Force.

"Things should be better once they get into the open, Mr. President. Our birds are fast enough they can't hide when we see 'em. Trouble is, as has been mentioned, they're almost impossible to see, especially from a distance. And we can't strafe and bomb our own cities."

"You're telling me the same thing everyone else is telling me!" Samuels shouted, losing control. "Are all of you saying we can't whip a bunch of God damn overgrown lizards?"

"Sorry, sir," Taffey said as others in the room avoided the President's glare. "We should do better once they're airborne."

"Damn it, Walter. Damn it all to hell! All I hear is 'sorry', 'should', 'maybe' and 'shucks'! What kind of talk is that? We've got a world on the line here, people. Whatever happened to words like 'will' and 'can' and 'win'?"

When nobody answered Samuels let his anger go. What was the point? He looked around the room, at the tired and angry faces. He sat down, pretended to read some notes of his own. When calm again, Samuels turned to his Secretary of Defense.

"Harold?"

"We're losing, sir. There's no other word for it. They eat everything in sight, including grass and milk cartons and everything a goat would eat. More, even. They're regular garbage cans. Our domestic livestock don't stand a chance, and neither do our people. These things have grown to huge proportions, and quick. So quick, in fact, they defy all the laws of nature. According to Professor Malfusco they may never stop growing, like fish in the sea. They're violent. They're strong. They break down your average house as if it were cardboard. We've even had reports they eat the damn two-by-fours! These things would put a T-Rex to shame, if there were any of them around."

"Are you telling me these things are invincible?" Samuels asked.

"No, sir. Nothing is invincible."

"Well, then, how do we get rid of them?"

"We need heavier firearms in the cities, Mr. President," General Cable started, then stopped. He cleared his throat. Realizing he had been in a slouch he straightened up and looked at Samuels.

"We've found flame throwers to be effective. When we can corner them, anyway. We'll need to use our arsenal of napalm, rockets, heavy artillery, cluster bombs. Everything we've got. Land mines. Saturation techniques. As Alex said, they've proven too fast for our ground troops. They see a tank, hear a shot, they're gone. We've had some sniper success with elephant guns and the lot, from far off, but that's a tough go. Unless you hit them in the eyes or ears the rounds are ineffective. The civilians are starting to do some damage, now that they realize what's going on. Those with the larger rifles, anyway, and those with outlawed weapons."

"Like what?" Samuels asked.

"Hand grenades, for one," the Secretary of Defense said. "Russian AK-47's, machine guns, bazookas, RPG's, you name it. We should never have passed those gun laws, Jack. Most of us here were against them, if you'll remember. We'd have a better chance now if our civilians had been allowed to retain their arms."

"We don't need hindsight here, Harold," Samuels said.

"The Secretary is right," the Marine Crops Commandant began . . .

"Look, all of you, " Samuels barked, feeling his anger rise again. "This is not the time for politics! Now, if you don't mind, let's stick to the business at hand!" Samuels turned his gaze on the General of the Air Force. "What about heat seeking missiles, Walter?"

"The Dragons don't generate enough heat, Mr. President. We've tried it. Sorry."

"Can't you modify the damn things?"

"The Dragons, sir? I don't understand."

"Jesus! The missiles, Walter. The missiles!"

Embarrassed, Taffey went on. "Yes, sir. We can. But it will take a lot of time."

"Walter, we don't have any time! That's what I've been trying to tell all of you here!"

"We're doing our best, Mr. President," Taffey said, becoming angry himself.

"Then your best is not good enough, General. Isn't that apparent by now?"

Taffey clenched his teeth and locked eyes with Samuels for a second, then looked away. He picked up a pencil and pretended to write something in his notebook. Others around the room did the same, not wanting to feel the heat that Taffey had taken. Samuels sighed and decided to change the topic.

"Have the inland cities been evacuated yet?" he asked, looking to his Secretary of the Interior.

"Sort of," Grayfeather answered, wishing the president had called on someone else.

"Damn it, Wanda, what the hell does that mean? Sort of?"

"The inland cities were evacuated, Jack, but now the refugees from the coastal towns are in them. It's like a flood, moving towards the spine of the continent. There's really no place to go. All the inland cities are now filled to overflowing. People seem to think they'll be safer there than out in the open. They're hiding out in basements, and silos, and concrete buildings. And they're all hungry, Jack. We don't have enough food to go around."

"Winter will be here soon, Mr. President," the Secretary of Agriculture, Ray Martinez, said. "Maybe the cold weather will slow them down.

"They're in Alaska, and Siberia. Iceland's gone, as far as we know," Adams said. "Cold weather doesn't seem to be bothering them that much."

Samuels grunted. He left his seat and paced up and down. As he paced his frustration slowly gave way to determination. After a few minutes he walked back to his seat and sat down.

"All right, people. Here's what we're going to do. I want fortifications set up around the major interior cities. Tanks, artillery, whatever. Snipers. Troops with the tanks. Battle lines, if you will, from which there will be no retreat. More soldiers on ranches and farms, in hiding, wherever you think these creatures will strike. Above all I want our interior cities protected. Those with, say, a quarter million or more in population. Set them up as refugee camps. Start enlisting anyone able to fight into the ranks. If we're going down, we're going down fighting. Understood?"

"Yes, sir," a chorus of voices said, glad to have a plan.

"General Taffey, I want your planes in the sky at all times. Yours too, Admiral Peronski. All our helicopters, too. I want our ground troops to force those things into the air, and I want our air forces to destroy them when they get there. Poison cattle and sheep and leave them around for bait. Gas them. I don't care what you do, but we've got to do it quick. Understood?"

Another chorus of voices.

"And our cities, Mr. President?" Adams asked. "The ones with both civilians and Dragons in them?"

"Destroy them. Burn 'em down. Do whatever it takes. We don't want these damn things getting any farther inland if we can help it."

"But, sir . . .?

"Damn it, man, didn't you just tell me we were losing this war?"

"Yes, sir, but . . . "

"You ought to know me by now, Harold. And the rest of you, too. I don't like losing. If half of us have to die before we stop these things, well, that's better than all of us dying, isn't it? Sacrifices are just going to have to be made. And if any of you think I like this, you're crazier than I know you to be. I have family out there, too. Now, let's get on with it. Time is of the utmost importance here. We've got to gain control before our supplies are exhausted. I want half of Malfusco's Dragons taken out in the next twenty-four hours. Anything short of this goal will be unacceptable. Afterwards we'll concentrate on the rest. We've got a world to save here, people. We've done it before, and we can damn well do it again."

"Jack, can't we warn the people first?" Grayfeather protested. "Drop leaflets, or something?"

"Wanda, we don't have the time! The Dragons will be airborne soon. We've got to stop them now, in the trenches, before they take to the air. It may be our last chance. I'll see what the TV and radio people can do, but with communications down in most cities I don't think they'll have much luck."

"This is all so much crap," Leandra Knight, the President's Secretary of Urban Affairs, said, siding with Grayfeather. Sensitive to a fault, the youngest cabinet member was close to tears. "Killing our own people. There has to be a better way."

"I wish there were," Samuels said, his heart going out to her. He knew the rest of his people had relatives scattered around the States, same as he did. But there was nothing he could do other than what he was doing. Knight slumped in her chair, then threw her pencil at the far wall as hard as she could.

"Twenty-four hours is not much time, Jack," Cable said, staring at the pencil which had stuck in a picture of George Washington.

"It's all you're getting, General. And if you're telling me you can't do this . . .if *any* of you are telling me you can't do this . . . then please, let me know and I'll find the people who can!"

General Cable frowned. He looked at his fellow officers, then back to

Samuels.

"We'll get it done, Jack. You can count on us."

"Good! Glad to hear it. I want progress reports from all of you, every four hours, on the dot. On anything and everything. Now, let's get going. I'll be damned if I'm going to get my ass kicked by a bunch of flying horned toads!"

After they'd all left, after he was sure no one could see or hear, the President of what was left of the United States walked into the bathroom, shut the door behind him and held back the tears as long as he could.

Chapter 15
Captured

Back at the hotel Marsha scrutinized the pizza Jacob had ordered.

"I'm not hungry," she said. "People are dying out there, Jake. All over the world. Probably starving by now, and here we are, drinking beer and eating pizza. What the hell is that?"

"You have to eat," Jacob reprimanded, though he wasn't all that hungry himself. "You can't do battle on an empty stomach."

"What battle? No one's asked my opinion in all this. I feel like I'm holding your shirt tail. I want to go home."

"All right then. What's *your* opinion?"

"Thanks for asking, Professor. I think your Dragons are but the first wave of a bigger invasion. Once the Dragons have beaten everything down the real villains will move in and take over. Earth will be exhausted, and we'll have no pizzazz left to fight back."

"Pizzazz?"

"You know what I mean."

"The alien astronaut theory?"

"What else could it be? That's better than your 'relic' theory, which, in case you haven't noticed, has been blown all to hell."

Jacob shrugged. "If what you say is true, then why didn't the real villains take over the world the last time they were here? Or the time before? They would have certainly had an easier time of it, don't you think?"

"We don't know that. Maybe conditions weren't right. It was the end of a very cold glacial period, after all. It has something to do with humanity, Jake, but I haven't figured it out yet."

"Well, let me know when you do."

"I want to go home, Jacob."

"Damn it, Marsha, don't start again! Read my lips. *There is no home!*"

"I'll go it alone, then! I can take care of myself!"

"Then go on!" Jacob shouted. "I'm tired of listening to it!"

When Marsha made ready to leave Jacob jumped off the bed and stood between her and the door. He put his hands on her shoulders.

"Look, sweetheart, we have to see this thing through," he said, searching her eyes. "And this is the best place to do it. You know that! If we're to have any chance at all it's right here. Why can't you understand that?"

Marsha returned Jacob's stare for a moment, then cast her eyes to the ground. She began to tremble.

"Oh, Jake," she said, wrapping her arms around his waist. She nestled her head on his chest as tears welled up and rolled from her eyes. "What's to become of us? Our beautiful world?"

"C'mon, baby," Jacob murmured as he stroked her hair. "Crying's not going to help anything."

"I want to see my daughter. I need to know that she's all right."

Jacob sighed. He unwrapped Marsha's arms from around his waist and sat down beside her. "How about I fix you a drink? A nice, stiff one. Then we'll talk."

"All right," Marsha answered. She wiped at her eyes with a corner of the bed spread. Jacob got up and mixed himself a scotch and soda and his wife a double whiskey seven. They had taken to drinking again prior to doomsday, but not as heavy as before, and only on occasion. He gave Marsha her drink and turned on the TV.

"I thought we were going to talk."

Jacob pointed at his watch. "It's noon. Time for the news."

"I don't want to watch the news! There's nothing good on it anymore."

"It'll only be a minute. I promise. Then we'll talk. Enjoy your drink."

Marsha pouted.

"Honey, we have to know what's going on, don't we?"

"I don't care anymore, Jake. Read *my* lips!"

"Well I do! Just give me a minute. Now drink up and I'll make you another."

Jacob turned on the tube as Marsha stuck her finger in her glass and twirled the ice. Once he had the right channel Jacob relaxed back on the bed. They watched as the familiar face, becoming more haggard with each broadcast, came onto the screen.

". . . show that Japan has been completely overrun, along with North and South Korea. Taiwan is gone. All the islands. Australia is on its way, although they have heavily fortified positions they are defending, apparently with some success. Millions of people have died. Maybe hundreds of millions by now. As reports from the overrun countries continue to dwindle, we have no way of knowing for sure. England is gone as far as we know though, at last report, they are holding out in certain cities, same as Australia. Further reports coming in show mass starvation . . ."

Jacob turned the TV off.

"A hundred million dead? Unbelievable. And only fifteen or so million Dragons? That's what? Six people a day per Dragon? Not to mention all the pigs and cows. That's a pretty healthy appetite."

"Jesus Christ, Jake! How can you talk about it so flippantly? Those are people out there. Real people. It's not some God damn movie you're watching, where everything turns out dandy at the end!"

"I'm not being flippant!"

"The hell you're not!" Marsha shouted. She got up off the bed. "Watch your stupid TV. I'm going for a walk."

"Wait a minute!" Jacob said as Marsha opened the door and stalked out, drink still in hand. "It's not safe out there!"

Marsha was halfway down the hallway when Jacob made it to the door.

Let her go, Jacob, he said to himself. *This being cooped up together is getting on your nerves anyway.*

He watched as Marsha vanished down the stairwell, then went back inside and shut the door. After a couple slices of pizza and another scotch Jacob lay down on the bed and was soon asleep. Two hours later a jangling telephone woke him up.

"The President wants to see you, Mr. Malfusco," the urgent voice said. "Right away. We've got a Dragon at The Mountain he wants you to look at."

Jacob told the man he would be there as soon as he could. He found Marsha a block away, drinking at a bar with several military men. When Jacob told her of the call she came willingly enough. Jacob bought her some strong coffee at a corner 7-11 and soon they were on their way.

"Shorry for the way I acted," Marsha said halfway there, her speech slurred by too many drinks. She patted Jacob on the leg and giggled. His girl had been doing good, Jacob reflected. Until lately. Hopefully she wouldn't become an alcoholic again. He wondered how many drinks she'd had. Not that he should talk. He was back to smoking five or six cigars a day since the Dragons had come ashore. This after having quit for all that time. He was angry with himself, and Marsha, too, but what difference did it make? If he was going to end up in some Dragon's soup, or starving to death, what did it matter?

* * *

An hour and a half after the call they were at Cheyenne Mountain. A military officer at the gate checked their ID and then escorted the Malfuscos to a large, rectangular building outside The Mountain. Once inside they joined up with a dozen other people, mostly military. The room they ended up in was an old hangar, cold and austere, without windows, but well lighted. Off in one corner a helicopter rested. There was an antiseptic smell about the place, like a hospital operating room. On a series of strung together, heavy duty tables, towards the center of the room, lay the slain Dragon. On inquiry Jacob found it had been lowered by crane through a roof that opened and shut. Its color was gone, and so was the fire from its open eyes. Jacob could see a series of large wounds to the chest and belly. Dried, red blood all but covered the beast, and pools of it lay on the tables.

"My God, it's twice as big as the ones we first saw," Marsha gasped, sober now in the cold air and within touching distance of the Dragon.

"It's enormous," Jacob said in awe, unable to view the entire bulk of the animal from where he stood. "And look at the wings. I'd guess they were fully developed, or close to it."

"I'm Doctor Bellinger," a tall, thin, stringy-haired brunette said, extending her hand to Jacob. She wore a white surgeon's gown, smeared with more blood. The doctor ignored Marsha, just a cursory nod in her direction. "We'd like you to take a look, tell us what you think, where it might be most vulnerable."

Jacob walked slowly around the beast, Marsha beside him. Together they scrutinized and, along with Bellinger and several others, they poked, prodded and punched. After several minutes Jacob saw something he hadn't seen on the juveniles; a large, empty, apparently deflated sack, starting below the jaw bone and working its way down the underside of the neck for a couple of feet.

"What's this?" Jacob asked, holding the sack in both hands and running his fingers over it. The skin was cold and clammy, not unlike a dead fish. The sack was covered with small scales and, like the rest of the Dragon, was of a dead, gray color.

"We were hoping you would tell us," an Air Force colonel said. An hour later they were no closer to the mystery of the pouch than they had been earlier.

"Beats me," Jacob said. "I'm sorry. I'm not a doctor. Doctor of medicine, anyway. Looks like it might be a storage pouch. You know, like the marsupials have? The kangaroos? Maybe it's a kind of hump, like camels have. For storing water. Maybe food."

"Its most vulnerable points?" the colonel asked.

"The mouth, eyes, ears, underbelly. The anus. The wings and legs at the joints. You won't kill them there but they'll certainly be hobbled. Maybe the head plate if it's blown off. The tail, too. Injure that significantly and I doubt it'll be able to fly. Other than that, with those armor like scales, the average bullet is not going to penetrate."

"Or spear, or arrow," Marsha offered.

"We'll hope it doesn't come to that," one of the doctors said.

"What brought this one down?" Jacob asked.

"One of our Marine squads brought it down with several RPG's," A Marine Corps major said. "Like you guessed, small arms are useless, and the larger weapons like mortars and bazookas, say, are hard to focus on something that moves so quickly. Using heavy artillery is a crap shoot. We've got a lot of problems but, as you can see, we're making some progress. From our estimates we've taken out maybe fifty thousand so far, here in the States. Mostly with choppers."

That's all? Jacob couldn't help but think. *Out of millions?*

* * *

"They're grasping at straws, Marsha," Jacob said on the way home. "That's why they called us there. We're losing this thing, and we're losing bad."

"They called *you* there."

"Whatever."

The Malfuscos arrived back at their hotel room around eleven that night. After dinner and cocktails on the government, they slept fitfully, or not at all.

Chapter 16
Night of the Dragon

The fourth day of the invasion found the world on the brink of collapse. Cities and towns across the globe were in flames, while their citizens cowered in caves and basements, or headed away from the coasts as fast as their vehicles, or legs, could carry them. Vast streams of humanity crowded the roads, hoping to find sanctuary inland. The Dragons had moved through and out of the coastal cities and towns, gathering strength and size as they moved east or west. The smaller islands around the globe were now depleted of food for the most part. Those people who had survived the initial onslaught were beginning to feel the first pangs of real hunger. They began to fight over what was left, killing each other in the process, making easy pickings for insatiable Dragons. Gone were the cattle and sheep, the pigs and chickens, bananas, late corn and rice. Feeling the pull of distant horizons, the Dragons made ready to move off the islands and join their brothers and sisters on the mainlands of Earth.

At ten P.M., as the world turned, the Dragons ceased to hunt and rested for the night. Their skin was the color of whatever lay about them. They were hard to see, and harder to find. Wings developed fully as night progressed, scales became stronger, brains engineered for survival in the harshest of climates became fine tuned. Empty neck pouches began filling with a mixture of methane and other gasses, metabolized from Dragon waste products and stored there. Juvenile teeth fell out and were replaced by longer, more effective, razor sharp canines and fangs. Four of the smaller teeth up front formed flint like caps that, when ground together, emitted sparks that ignited the gaseous mixture on contact with oxygen. Long trails of fire were the end result, thrown forward with the velocity of a flame thrower, Dragon anger the catalyst. The claws grew longer and sharper, curved like those of an eagle, made for grasping, and tearing, and perching on anything that would hold their weight. Dragon feet would not be needed as much for walking, but more for attacking from the air, more for holding onto prey while in flight. The Dragons rested, and grew, and became more formidable with each passing hour.

In the early morning light, minutes before sunrise, the island Dragons, full blown adults, opened their eyes and stretched, then took flight towards the mainlands, towards whichever continent lay closest to them. There they would join their brethren in a never-ending quest for food. They filled the skies, flying in huge, wedge shaped formations, so thick in places they blotted out the sun, and their cries of hunger and helplessness filled the air.

Chapter 17
Yokosuka, Japan

Kiego Matsuburu gazed out over the broken landscape, tears in his eyes and in his heart. Heavy smoke from a thousand fires filled the air.

"Maybe Hiroshima and Nagasaki not so bad as this, neh?" he said to the man standing next to him, Hiro Sumida. Friends and neighbors for ages, both in their early seventies, they were hungry, dirty, bruised, cut and angry.

"They have gone now," Hiro said, kicking at the pile of ash where his home had stood but days before. "We must rebuild."

"Our paper and wood homes were no match for them," Kiego said. "We have nothing left."

"*We* are left. There are others. We must rebuild."

"With what, Hirosan? We can expect no help from other countries this time."

"There is talk of a young girl in Oppama who has befriended one of the Dragons. Have you heard?" Hiro asked, changing the subject.

"Yes. I have heard there are others, too, but it is hard to believe."

"It follows her through the streets like a dog."

"People are not afraid?"

"Rumor has it they are not. They feed it what they can, and it responds like a pet. A cross between a cat and a dog, perhaps. They see it as a sign of good fortune."

"Fortune? After all that has happened? Surely they must destroy it."

"They say it saved the girl, and many others, from its own kind. They say it saved the town. What was left of it, anyway."

"Amazing. I hear it recovered from severe wounds in less than a day."

"An awesome animal. Like those from our past, neh?"

"What will they do with it? Surely their food supplies are gone, as are ours."

"They will have no choice but to kill it for meat, I am afraid. I wonder what Dragon steaks taste like?"

"Do you think they will return?"

Hiro stared eastward, through the smoke and to the ash covered hills, over which the Dragons had flown but hours earlier. Then he fell to his knees, his mind rebelling, and buried his face in his hands. Kiego knelt down beside his lifelong friend and covered him with his only jacket, then felt the horrible cold of an early winter creeping along his skin.

Chapter 18
Oahu, Hawaii

Air force Major John Quincy Reynolds peered out from the small window
on the north side of the concrete bunker. Hickam Air Force Base had been
under siege for four days now. The small Hawaiian island resembled a war
zone, as did all the other islands in the chain. Honolulu was on fire, and so
were all the other island towns. Smoke billowed into the air and drifted out
to sea, pushed along this morning by a mild trade wind. All about lay torn
and twisted steel, remnants of planes, hangars and military equipment.
Reynolds thought this must be the way Pearl Harbor looked, back when the
Japanese had run their sneak attacks.

The sun was rising along the eastern horizon. Bright rays of gold split an
intense blue sky where they could be seen behind the smoke. The major, a
slight, well-muscled, handsome man, was crammed into the World War II
structure with twenty-two soldiers and civilians, all, as far as he knew, that
was left of Hickam's population. There were no children. He ate slowly from
a can of peaches that would be his only meal of the day. Canned fruit and
vegetables were about all they had left, and they were fast running out of
those. Reynolds wondered how they were going to survive when the food
ran out. There would be no help from the States, of that he was sure. At least
not for a while. Somehow they were going to have to find a way to rid the
islands of the Dragons. But how? If they tried to leave the bunker they were
attacked within minutes. Too many people had already been lost to try that
again.

Communications were down. Had been since day two. Reynolds suspected
that things were as bad around the globe as they were on Oahu. At the onset
he and some of his fellow pilots had flown several sorties against the invaders,
with some success. Three of his men had been trapped, and killed, on the
second day running for their airplanes. Somehow the Dragons had caught
on. They had keen eyes and ears, and attacked anything that moved, including
jets taxiing on the runways. Or coming to rest after landing.

After the first day the major and his men never had a chance. Using Jeeps
and Hum-Vees to run for the planes had proved futile too, easily turned over

by the huge Dragons. The men, and the women, inside them had been extracted and eaten. The Dragons rested at night, he knew, but when you couldn't see them, what good did that do? Night goggles might be useful, if they had any of the damn things. Were he not a military man he would have deemed the situation hopeless.

Reynolds was pondering how to get his squadron back into the air when an excited airman rushed into the room.

"Sir!" Molly shouted, talking as she saluted. "Major Reynolds! They're leaving!"

"What?" Reynolds said, almost choking on his peaches. Molly had the attention of everyone in the room. "Who's leaving? I gave strict orders for everyone to stay put!"

"The Dragons, sir. They're flying away! Headed east, towards the States."

Reynolds put down his peaches and ran up the steps to the bunker hatchway. He opened it a crack, just in time to see several hundred of the beasts flying over the island. Reynolds opened the door farther and took a quick summary of the area. There were no Dragons on the ground that he could see. But that didn't mean much. They blended in so well with their surroundings you couldn't see them half the time anyway.

Reynolds threw caution to the wind and opened the door half way. Over the water, a mile or so out, he saw another cluster of the damn things flying towards the States. From his bunker they looked like a large flock of Canadian geese on the wing, but they were way too big to be geese.

"They're going away, sir!" Molly said, having come up the steps and peering over his shoulder.

"I can see that, Bochey," Reynolds said. He opened the hatch all the way and scrutinized the area. It took him only seconds to make his decision.

"Bochey, go back below and get everyone on the tarmac. Order a scramble. We're going on a Dragon hunt, airman. It's payback time."

"Yahoo!" Molly shouted as she ran back down the steps.

* * *

Thirty minutes later Reynolds and seven other pilots, all that were left, were in hot pursuit of the airborne Dragons. Quick on land, the Dragons were relatively slower in the air. At least flying horizontally. Once up the Dragons soared with the air currents, gliding along like giant albatrosses high above the blue-green Pacific. They flapped their wings only when necessary to give them added lift, and their highly maneuverable tails and head plates kept them easily in the currents. Flying along at less than fifty miles per hour, their slowness and maneuverability proved a major handicap for the supersonic jets.

Reynolds and the pilots with him, five men and two women, split into groups of four and took off after the two separate clusters of Dragons. Diving from above, out of the sun, and flying faster than the speed of sound they caught the alien invaders completely by surprise. After that, however, they scored very few hits. The Dragons broke formation, dove and flew low to the water, separating from each other as they skimmed the waves, going in all directions. In minutes their skin became the color of the ocean. The pilots could only track them by their shadows on the surface. When one of the pilots would begin his or her dive to strafe one of the beasts the Dragon would simply reverse course. The jets moved too fast to make such quick maneuvers, even when they had slowed to minimum airspeed, and more often than not found their ammunition impacting nothing but the ocean's surface. One pilot slowed too much, stalled, and slammed into the Pacific. Two others died while diving on a single shadow from opposite directions, unable to get out of each other's way. Reynolds called it quits. Everyone had lost heart, and fuel was getting low.

"Damn it," Reynolds cursed on his way back to Hickam. "I'm sure people stateside don't need more Dragons landing on their doorsteps."

* * *

Flying over Oahu, Reynolds found a devastated island. Lines were down, cities were in flames, there were no signs of life. Sugar cane and pineapple fields had been trampled. On landing he found the island's terrified survivors still afraid to come out of hiding, even when the remaining military personnel told them it was safe.

"What if they come back?" was the most common question.

When the final tally was in Oahu had lost over eighty percent of its civilian population, and close to ninety percent of its military. The rest of the island chain had lost similar amounts and food supplies were down to meager rations, or none at all. As bad as it was, compared to most of the other islands around the world, the Hawaiians came through smelling like roses.

At approximately six P.M. that evening Major Reynolds and elements of Hawaii's Pacific Command set sail for the west coast of the United States, there to join the Third Fleet out of San Diego, and the Seventh Fleet steaming over from Japan. They weren't sure they could accomplish anything, but they had to try. All the firepower of all the world's naval vessels weren't much good against land going creatures, and trying to knock one out of the air with a ship's cannon was a lesson in foolhardiness. They had to fly towards you first, and there had yet to be a confirmed report of Dragons attacking ships or submarines. Why, no one knew. Two hours later America's remaining three fleets, those in the Mideast, Indian Ocean and the Mediterranean, set sail for home. America was in desperate straights, and the rest of the world was going to have to fend for itself.

Chapter 19
Dissension

Sunday morning dawned clear and cold. The Malfuscos, overwhelmed from their four-day ordeal, slept past the hour they had wanted to get up. Outside their sixth story hotel room a strong wind furrowed down the canyons, then flattened out and covered Colorado Springs with bone chilling gusts. It was the beginning of an early winter, but nobody noticed. They had other things on their mind.

Inside The Mountain Jack Samuels bit into a sweet roll, chewed, then washed it down with some strong black coffee. Like Marsha, he felt guilty. Here he was, with plenty to eat and drink, in a fortress that was impossible to penetrate, and his nation was in chaos. Samuels' head drooped. He was beginning to feel incompetent and useless, emotions he'd never experienced before. He was his country's leader, wasn't he? Elected by the people to protect them, keep them out of harm's way? It was up to him to get everyone out of this mess, and he was failing horribly. He knew the world was counting on him, too. The President was not a happy man.

Samuels righted his head and took another swig of coffee. He surveyed the room and his weary staff, then looked towards General Cable.

"What do you have for me this morning, Aaron?" he managed.

"I'm afraid nothing good, Jack."

"Go on."

"They've flown over our fortifications, Mr. President. All of them. Right over and into the cities we're trying to protect. We took some out, but hey flew too high for our artillery, and then dove in on the cities. Our pilots did some damage, but we don't have near enough to go around, and, ironically, our fighter planes are proving too fast to be effective. To compound the matter we're getting low on fuel. A lot of our refineries have been destroyed and, without oil from our overseas suppliers, we'll be running out soon."

Samuels drank more coffee, ran a hand through unwashed hair. "What about you, Walter?" he asked the Air Force general, a man he had served under during the Muslim Wars, and had the greatest respect for.

"About the same thing, Mr. President. They've learned to fly very low, or very high. Apparently they have great lung capacity to go along with everything else. When they're against the sky they turn the color of that sky. When they're on the ground they turn the color of that ground. Our pilots are searching for shadows to shoot at, and that's a very difficult thing to do. Unfortunately, in the process, some of our pilots have mistaken aircraft shadows for Dragon shadows from time to time."

"What does that mean?"

"They've shot each other down, sir."

"Jesus Christ, Walter," Samuels said, shaking his head. "Jesus H. Christ."

"I'm sorry, Jack. We've never trained to fight like this. But I can assure you we're learning, and we're learning fast."

"That's good to know, Walter," Samuels said sarcastically. "Anything else?"

"Well, sir, looking for shadows wastes a lot of fuel, and these things don't fly all that much anyway," Taffey said carefully, not liking his President's tone. "Just enough to get from here to there. They still spend most of their time on the ground eating, I'm afraid, and we can't see them there. Not from the air."

"Can't you fly boys figure out something effective, General?" Samuels asked as a wave of frustration washed over him, "Isn't that what you guys are paid to do? Seems like a hell of a waste of time, money and lives if you people can't produce."

Taffey stiffened visibly. "You used to be a pilot, Jack. Maybe you should get back into the air and show the rest of us how it's supposed to be done."

"That's your job, Walter. Remember? That's why I asked for you in the first place! You keep telling me you can do this, and then nothing happens! How about the truth for a change?"

"Damn it, Jack! We're doing the best we can. If you people hadn't cut military spending so much maybe we wouldn't be in this mess. Bases closed, ships decommissioned, aircraft grounded. Not to mention the stricter gun laws. *Your* ideas Jack. Not mine!"

Samuels reddened. He was about to speak, to scream, to dismiss all of his incompetent military chiefs when Magdalena Dominguez, his Secretary of Labor, interrupted.

"Gentlemen, gentlemen!" she said, standing up from her seat down the table. She slapped the table repeatedly with the flat of her hand. "This is not getting us anywhere! This is not what we are here for! Now, either we proceed in a calm and dignified manner or I, for one, am leaving. We do not need this.

Not now. Especially not now, when Americans are counting on us! So, if you will pardon me, what is it going to be here? You are acting like spoiled children!"

General Taffey calmed himself. He looked first to Dominguez, then to Samuels.

"Sorry sir," he said, and his tone was firm and controlled. "Sorry Maggy. I'm out of line here. It's just that nobody seems to understand what we're up against. Everything has happened so fast . . ."

Samuels let out air he didn't know he'd been holding. He waved his hand towards the general, dismissing the incident. "Forget it, Walter. Our Secretary of Labor is right, as always. And we're tired here." He looked towards Dominguez. "And thanks, Maggy. I promise to proceed on a calmer note."

Dominguez bit her lip and nodded, then sat back down. "We are going to hold you to it, Mr. President," she said, then bowed her head and crossed herself. Others around the room relaxed a little.

Samuels nodded, gazed into an empty cup. "Admiral Peronski?" he said, turning his attention towards his Fleet Admiral.

"We have the Third Fleet stationed up and down the coast, assisting where we can, Mr. President. Helping the wounded and hungry, using it to launch and land aircraft along with other things, as you ordered. The rest of our ships are on their way home. Hopefully they'll be here within a week or two."

"Good. We need all the help we can get, Admiral."

"Understood, sir."

"General Jackson?" Samuels said, turning to look at his Commandant of the Marine Corps.

"Our aircraft are having the same problems as the others, Mr. President, but I do have a bright note. Our helicopter squadrons are doing well. And not just ours. All the services. They're able to maneuver with the Dragons, and can get close enough to the creatures for our weapons to be effective. Sometimes, anyway. So far they've been our best line of defense, both in the cities and the country. We're in the air constantly. Unfortunately, as you've probably guessed, we don't have enough helos to go around. And the Dragons fight back. They've flown right into our birds, knocking them out of the air. We don't know if it's because they think they can get to the pilots for a meal, or if it's just a defensive reaction. Whatever the case, we *are* bringing them down. Our ground forces are starting to have some effect, especially in the dark using night vision devices. We've been working in concert with the

Army and National Guard, but there's a lot of Dragons, we're stretched pretty thin, and our fuel reserves are low. But we're getting there, sir," he added, wishing there was some truth to his last sentence.

"Thank you, General," Samuels said, perking up some. "Keep up the good work. Anybody else have something to say before we wrap up here?"

"I have some news, Jack," Cina Chang, the President's Attorney General, said. The striking Asian woman stood up, all four-feet ten of her, so that the others might better hear her. Chang smiled briefly, then turned her eyes on the President. She paused, not sure how to say what she had to say.

"Well, what is it?" Samuels asked after a few seconds, anxious to get on with the day.

"I have received some scattered reports from the Far East, Jack. India, China, Japan. All Asiatic countries. So far, anyway. The information is not concise. In fact, it may be wishful thinking, but I thought you might like to hear it."

"Cina, get on with it, would you?"

"Yes, sir. Well, as strange as this may sound, the information I have received suggests that several people, in different places, have made pets of these Dragons." The President, as well as several others around the room, burst into laughter, but it was cut short when a wounded look crossed Chang's face.

"Cina, please," Samuels said, shaking his head, "we don't have time for fairy tales here. Or wishful thinking. You can't be serious?"

"Jack, it's true! They all follow the same pattern. Some person stumbles upon a wounded Dragon and feeds and nurses it. All of them have been children, by the way. I doubt adults would approach a disabled Dragon. They'd probably shoot it first. Anyway, the person befriends it. Apparently the Dragon becomes attached, like a stray dog or cat does when you feed it. They even protect the person against other Dragons, should the need arise."

"That sounds pretty farfetched," the President's Chief of Staff, Martin Davis said. Oldest man in the room, the chief was well known for his skepticism.

"Well, Marty," Cina returned, "it may well be. But let me clarify something here. I won't take but a minute, Jack. Dragons have always played an important part in Oriental history. They're an integral part of our culture. I'm sure you know this. What you may not know is that, unlike Dragons in western cultures that are portrayed as evil beasts, Oriental Dragons have been portrayed, down through the centuries, as both evil *and* good."

"No, I wasn't aware of that," Davis said. "So you think these reports are true? That Dragons can be tamed?"

"Exactly what I'm saying. We know Dragons have been on Earth before. Perhaps it's time to try a different tact here."

"You mean hand feed the devils?" Magdalena Dominguez, incredulous, asked from across the table.

"Something like that."

"Thanks, but you can leave me out."

"Me, too," several others around the room echoed.

"I'll do that," Chang said, becoming irritated at her cohorts' attitudes.

"And if these rumors are false?" General Cable scoffed. "What then?"

"Can't we at least try?" Chang asked. "What have we got to lose?"

"An arm, a leg, a head," Dominguez said.

Often at odds with one another, Samuels cut in before Chang and Dominguez could tear into each other.

"Craziest thing I've heard, Cina," he said, glaring at Dominguez. "But no thanks. I don't see how we can start adopting, and feeding, these damn things. We don't have enough food to feed our own people. And, along with General Cable, I don't see how we can take the chance. Sorry."

"Just thought you needed to know," Chang said. Unhappy with the results of her plea, she sat back down and studied her notes.

"We'll look into it, Cina. I promise," Samuels said. "Now, anything else?" he asked, looking around. When nobody spoke Samuels turned his attention to the Marine guard stationed inside the entrance door.

"Sergeant," he said, "would you mind opening the door and letting the others in now? Thank you. And I caution all of you not to mention what we've spoken of here. We don't need our top advisors to panic, or lose heart."

Samuels sighed and, head down, waited for his invited guests to enter. Hopefully, his top scientists and other key personnel would have some answers. An hour later, the President of the United States found himself shocked and severely disappointed.

Chapter 20
The Harvesters

After the President's select group of scientists and advisors had entered the room the sergeant closed the door and stood at parade rest.

"Good morning, and thank you all for coming," Samuels said, having stood up when the others entered. He watched as they took their accustomed places around the room. "I'm hoping you people will have some good news for us. Please, step forward if you have any information you think will help. Our time is short, but let me reassure all of you that our war against the invaders is going well. Now, do any of you have any information?"

Papalov Darringer stepped forward from the group of thirty or so people that lined the walls. He raised his hand.

"Your name, sir?" Samuels asked, sitting back down.

"Doctor Papalov Darringer, Mr. President. From the Mount Palomar Observatory in California."

"Yes, Dr. Darringer. I remember. You're the man that discovered the meteors. Am I correct?"

"Yes, sir."

"Good. Glad you're here. What do you have for me?"

"Early this morning I received news from my colleagues that they've discovered more, well, objects, headed towards Earth. In a different direction than the meteors came from. I thought you and your staff should be informed."

"You're damn right we should be informed!" the President said, shocked, as was everyone else in the room. It took a few seconds for Samuels to gather his wits, then: "You mean to tell me there are more of these damn things coming here? What the hell for? As a mop up crew? And how is it that you still have people on Palomar, Doctor? Not that I'm not glad! I thought that area was overrun days ago?"

"It was, sir. There weren't that many people there. It's rather isolated, and they were well prepared. Most of them survived. Anyway, these objects are different. They aren't eggs, if you will. They're large. Immense, even, and . . ."

"Go on."

"Well, sir, did you ever see the movie *Independence Day?*"

"As a matter of fact I did. Why?"

"These things headed our way, they're coming from the direction of Orion. Almost the same trajectory as the meteors. These objects aren't as big as the ones in the movie, but they're pretty close. Huge. And they travel in a V formation. Like geese traveling south. Or Dragons headed west."

"Do you have a count?" General Cable asked, his heart in his throat. "There aren't millions of them, are there?"

"As near as we can tell there are thirty-six," Darringer answered, turning to face the general.

"What are you saying here?" Samuels asked. "Get to the point."

Darringer turned back to face the President. "I believe they're space ships, sir."

"What?"

"There's nothing else they could be, when you think about it. They're coming to take our planet, and they've sent the Dragons to clear the way for them. We figure, at their present rate of speed, they should be here in three and one-half months, or around Christmas."

No one spoke for a while, lost in their own thoughts, too stunned to speak. Marsha Malfusco, standing towards the back with Jacob, her hair a mess and without makeup, took a hesitant step forward, raised her hand, then backed off.

"Jesus Christ," General Cable said after a few minutes, breaking the silence. "Jesus Christ and Holy Mother. And we've used up most of our arsenal fighting the damn Dragons. What are we supposed to do now?"

Chapter 21
Jump Start

"You sure those things are space ships?" Samuels asked of Darringer. "I mean, I thought interstellar travel was presumed impossible? Light speed and all."

"Apparently we've presumed wrong, Mr. President."

"Any chance they might be friendly?"

"I suppose anything's possible, but then, if that's the case, why send the Dragons?"

Samuels rose from his chair and paced up and down for a few moments, then he returned to the head of the table and sat back down. This certainly changed things. He thought of dismissing his civilian advisors but decided against it. They had a right to know his plans. Especially now. Fighting back feelings of rage, hopelessness and despair, the President spoke to his audience. He didn't stand up. He didn't want them to see that his hands were shaking.

"All right people, here's what we're going to do," he began, his jaw set. "We're going to rearm our nuclear missiles and activate the ones still armed. Somebody, some *thing*, wants my planet and, by God, as long as Jack Samuels is alive, they're not going to get it! We've got three months to prepare. I want the military to start bombing the cities. All of them that the Dragons are presently inhabiting. Start bombing the cattle farms, anywhere we think these things might be feeding, even if you can't see them. Blow everything all to hell. Use napalm, bunker busters, whatever it takes, short of nuclear weapons. We'll save those for the bastards in the ships. People, I'm sorry. I don't know what's going on here. I don't know why we're being picked on, why one race of intelligent beings would want to destroy another. What I do know is they can't have my planet! Not without a fight, anyway. We'll make them wish they'd never seen Earth! Now, are there any questions? Be brief. We need to get moving here."

"But, sir," Wanda Grayfeather protested, "there are still millions of people in those cities. What about them? What about the children?"

"I know that, Wanda! We've been all over this. If we're going to have a chance then we've got to take out these Dragons before they destroy any more of our infrastructure. And that means using everything at our disposal. I'm sorry about the civilians. I have family and friends in those cities, too. We all do. But it's better that some of us live than none of us, isn't it? You can't argue with that. And if you do, I won't listen. Aaron, order the military out of the cities. Heavy bombing and fire should bring the Dragons out. We'll catch them on the run, before they have time to adjust. The invaded cities have blockades around them, right?"

"Yes, sir. For the most part."

"All right then. Let's do it. You're all excused. I'd like my cabinet to meet back here in one hour, my military personnel in two. Thank you all for coming."

Marsha, afraid of being left out again, let go of Jacob's hand and stepped forward. She raised her hand.

"I, I have something to add, Mr. President. I think, well, I think we're way off base here."

"Oh?" the President said as all eyes turned to Marsha. Those that had risen out of their seats sat back down. "And who might you be, young lady?"

"I am Marsha Malfusco. Jacob Malfusco's wife. I, my daughter and I, we discovered the Uluru pyramid, over in Australia."

"I remember," Samuels said, irritated at the delay. Even though it was still morning, he needed a drink, and he needed it bad. "What is it you have to add?"

"We're hay, Mr. President," Marsha blurted. "We're the hay and the Dragons are the cattle. It's the only thing that makes sense here. We're not going to be invaded by people from another planet as Dr. Darringer is suggesting. It's something else."

"I'm not following you," Samuels said, wondering if he had some crackpot on his hands.

"It never occurred to me until Dr. Darringer said space ships were on their way. They're coming to harvest their Dragons, Mr. President. We're hay. Humans and everything else on the planet. Our home is very fertile. Always has been. Our world circles the sun in the right place, at the right time. It's a farm, and we're the farm animals. Us and the cattle and caribou, the fish and pigs and corn. Anything and everything edible."

"That's crazy," the Secretary of Defense said. "Why would anyone want to do something like that? The economics of traveling from one star system to another, even if you have faster than light speed, would be prohibitive. An advanced race of beings surely doesn't need to travel across the galaxy for food. They could well manufacture their own."

"Everyone likes a good steak," Marsha said to the man, having forgot his name. She smiled his way.

"I'm sorry?"

Marsha was about to explain her theory when the President's Chief of Staff cut her off.

"I'm sorry, Mrs. Malfusco, but we're short on time here. Do you have any, well, credentials to back up what you're saying?" he asked.

"What?"

"You know. College degrees, things of that nature."

Angry, Marsha spouted off her considerable list of credits. When she was through an embarrassed Chief of Staff apologized.

"I'm sorry, Mrs. Malfusco. The reason I asked is that I don't see your name on the list of invited guests. Can you explain that?"

"She's here with me," Jacob said, loud enough for everyone to hear. He glared at the Chief of Staff. "*I* invited her."

"All right, Mrs. Malfusco," Davis said, looking at Jacob. "That's good enough for me. You have the floor."

Red faced, Marsha continued. "Suppose these ships headed our way belong to a race of nomads, Mr. President? Space faring nomads. We know they've been here before. Everything in our past history, that's unexplained, points that way. The Dragons point that way. Suppose these people wander through space. Maybe they lost their home planet eons ago. Maybe they make a grand tour of all the inhabitable planets in our galaxy, or maybe just a few select ones, like Earth. Say they arrive here every nine thousand years or so. They release their cattle ahead of time, who devour everything in sight. When they mature our space farers gather them up for the next leg of their journey. By the time they come around again our world has recovered, and the cycle starts all over again."

Several people in the room stifled smiles. Others raised their eyebrows. General Cable laughed outright, but most of those present remained quiet, trying to comprehend what Marsha was saying.

"Please, go on," Samuels said after a minute or so. Intrigued, he had forgotten all his troubles for the moment.

"Think about it," Marsha said, locking eyes with Cable. "What happened here on Earth, eight, nine thousand years ago, General? Man became intelligent. There's been speculation as to why, so suddenly, for over a century now. These beings from outer space send their Dragons on ahead, give them a specified time to grow, then send their army in to harvest them."

"What you're saying is ludicrous, madam," Cable said. "If they ate everything in sight, there would be nothing left to repopulate our planet."

"But that's just it, General. They *don't* eat everything. They ravaged our oceans, but left enough of the zoo and phyto plankton, and smaller fishes, to repopulate there. They'll do the same on land. They won't get all the people, and they won't get all the deer."

"It's still ludicrous, ma'am," Cable said, on the defensive.

"Do you have a better idea, General? If so, I'd like to here it," Marsha said bluntly, challenging the man as she'd had to challenge so many before him.

"No. In all honesty I haven't had much time to think on such things, Mrs. Malfusco. I have a war to fight, remember?" Cable answered. He looked to Samuels for help. Marsha followed his eyes.

"Let's pick an arbitrary time, Mr. President," Marsha said. "Say eight, nine thousand years ago. Maybe earlier. Our friends flew in to harvest their crop. For the first time, on our planet, they discovered an animal with a brain. A large one. They lived in caves or mud huts or grass shacks. A few lived in the beginnings of crude cities. Our visitors decided to give us a little technology. Crop technology, medicinal technology. Pyramid technology, if you will . . ."

"Wait a minute here," Cable interrupted. "What do you mean 'For the first time'? Mrs. Malfusco? I'm no anthropologist but I've heard of Cro-Magnon men and women, and Neanderthal people. Why didn't your little green men jump start *them*? They were around a lot longer than nine thousand years ago, and *they* had big brains!"

"I have two explanations, General. The first is they didn't think we were ready. The second, the one I favor, is that they never noticed we were around. Science tells us that before the dawn of civilization there weren't too many people in the world. Some scientists put mankind's total population at not more than thirty thousand, world wide, at any given time before our revolution. And think about this: if *you* were a Cro-Magnon man and leader of a thirty-person tribe, say, and you saw space ships coming over the hill, what would *you* do? Run, that's what. And hide! Until they were gone. Early human beings weren't discovered because there weren't enough of us around at the time. As far as Neanderthal man goes, well, I think the Dragons did them in. How else could they disappear all at once?" Marsha paused and looked at Cable, savoring her victory before speaking again.

"Does that answer your question, General?" she asked shortly, smiling his way. Cable, shot down once again, could only look down at the table and nod his assent.

"Anyway, as I was saying," Marsha continued, "our visitors decided to give us a boost. Cities got started, Stonehenge and the pyramids came along a little later. Asperos. . ."

"Where's that? Asperos?" Cina Chang asked, butting in. "I never heard of it."

Marsha, ever patient in explaining her theories, turned to face the diminutive woman.

"It's a small city in Peru, outside of Nazca, where the lines are drawn, Ms. Chang. There are ancient mounds there, step pyramids. Very few people know about them. Sixty-five, seven thousand years old, give or take. They're small, and they're obscure, but they're there, nevertheless. These types of things, the pyramids and places like Stonehenge, they're all over the world. The pyramid I discovered in Australia has now been firmly dated at nine thousand years. God knows how many pyramids and Stonehenges remain to be discovered. There could be hundreds, maybe thousands, dating back to who knows when."

"Amazing," the President said as Marsha paused to catch her breath. "Would you like to come to the front, Mrs. Malfusco, where everyone can see you better?"

"No thanks. I'm about done here."

"Well, suit yourself."

Into it now, Marsha looked around the room and into the eyes of everyone who would meet hers. She waved her index finger at those higher ups seated at the table the way she liked to do in her classes at UCLA.

"Think about this now. All of you. If you look at it hard enough intelligence on Earth blossomed around seven thousand years ago as far as we can tell. I think it was earlier. But then, who am I? Right, Mr. Davis?"

The Chief of Staff, surprised at the question, furrowed his eyebrows and scratched his nose in reply. Marsha gave him her best 'Smart Ass' smile.

"Anyway," Marsha continued, "my question is 'How?' How was this accomplished all around the globe, and at approximately the same time? We were *given* our intelligence, as a lot of people have suggested down through the years. Oh, we had the beginnings. Cave paintings. Spears and arrows. Primitive wheat and corn, barley. There were the beginnings of cities, as I said. Like Mohenjo-Daro in Pakistan, the Sumerian cities along the Tigris and Euphrates in Arabia. Jericho. China and the Orient were getting started, as were the Americas, notably Mexico. No doubt we would have grown to the intelligence we enjoy today, but I am positive that it would have taken longer. Much, much longer. Thousands of years longer, perhaps. Mr. President, ladies and gentlemen, it is my opinion that the human race was jump started awhile back. Jump started to get us where we are today."

Marsha quit talking to let her speech settle in, but Samuels had a question to ask. Above the noise Marsha had generated he raised his hands and asked for quiet.

"I don't understand," Samuels said. "Exactly where *are* we today, Mrs. Malfusco?"

"There are billions of us, Mr. President. Billions of human beings on Mother Earth. Count us, if you can. We have proliferated like no other animal our world has known. We were given a jump start to assure an abundant supply of hay for the Dragons. We're third from the top in the alien food chain. Frankly, I think we exceeded their greatest expectations. Our world has more Dragon food on it than ever before. Thanks to us. Humanity."

"I still don't understand. Why would an alien race give us intelligence to the point where we're able to fight back? That doesn't make much sense to me."

"What she's saying," the Secretary of Defense said, beginning to grasp Marsha's theory, "is that we've exceeded their expectations in that respect. I don't think they expected us to be near this advanced in such a short time frame. Not that our so-called modern weapons seem to be mattering much."

"And how do you people account for George?" the President asked Marsha. "The Dragon your husband found? Last I heard he was seven thousand years old when he died, not nine. How do you account for the discrepancy?"

"I'll let Jacob answer that, Mr. President, if you don't mind." Marsha took the few steps necessary to grab Jacob's hand and pull him forward.

"He's a relic, Mr. President," Jacob said, looking at Samuels. He straightened himself and cleared his throat. "I wasn't sure at first, but I am now. For some reason he never made it to the train. Or more accurately, his parents didn't. Consider all the Dragons weren't harvested last time around. Crippled somehow, caught napping, late, whatever. Several are left behind, they breed, and the line continues. They hide, and they live a long time. But there's not very many of them to start with, and along comes man to hunt them down. Maybe my George was the last of his line in the Americas.

According to legend, St. George was supposed to have slain a Dragon around 300 A.D. Maybe *that* Dragon was the last of the European and Asian line."

"*If* he existed," Wanda Grayfeather said.

"I'm thinking he did," Jacob answered. "We just haven't found the skeleton."

"Sounds reasonable," Samuels said. He looked around the room. "Does anyone have any questions for these two? I certainly don't have an explanation of events. Maybe some of you have another idea?"

"So you're saying we've been invaded by Dragons for countless thousands of centuries?" General Cable asked, still refusing to believe.

"Yes," Jacob answered. "There have been die-outs on Earth for as long as it has been populated. Ten thousand or so years ago the mammoths died out, according to scientists. I'll bet it was closer to nine, the last time our Dragons made landfall, according to my wife's theory. Thirty thousand years ago it was the Neanderthals. Supposedly. I'll bet it was closer to twenty-seven, or thirty-six. Who knows what species of animals roamed our planet that the Dragons managed to wipe out? Or so depleted that they failed to survive? What about the dinosaurs? We're still guessing there. The list goes on."

"Do either of you have any idea where these ships might land?" Davis asked. "Any ideas at all?"

"I think I can pinpoint most of them," Marsha volunteered, looking at Davis. "Anywhere there's a pyramid, a Stonehenge, a Tassili or a Tiahuanoco. I can almost guarantee it."

Chapter 22
Going Home

There were tears of anger and frustration in Marsha's eyes on the way back to the hotel.

"The President's Chief of Staff is an asshole, you know that?" she said to Jacob as they turned a corner. Outside leaves and debris kicked up out of the gutters and hurried along the streets, pushed along by a late morning wind. Marsha wiped her eyes and blew her nose. "He asked for my 'credentials' in front of all those high falutin' people. What the hell was that? Embarrassed the pee out of me. Acted like I was some moron."

"I'm sure he didn't mean anything by it," Jacob said. He reached over and patted his wife on the leg.

"He's an asshole. And don't patronize me!"

* * *

Back in their room Marsha was inconsolable. Renewed tears ran down her face. She pulled out her various pieces of luggage and began packing.

"Now what are you doing?" Jacob asked. "We haven't been ordered out of here yet. Don't be doing something stupid here."

"Oh, wake up Jake," Marsha said. "Even if we beat the Dragons we can't fight those ships. Get a grip! I'm going home."

"Damn it, Marsha. We've gone over this before. Read my lips. *There ain't no home!*"

"My Trish is there, and parents are supposed to look after their children."

"You don't know she's there. And she's not a child."

"She's *my* child!"

"Jesus Christ, baby. Be sensible!"

Wiping at more tears, Marsha continued to pack. "If the reports are correct your Dragons are out of the coastal cities now. Or should be. I think we'll be safer there than here."

"And how do you propose to get there? Fly? Those things knock airplanes out of the sky. Or haven't you heard?"

"The Dragons aren't effective after sundown. I'm driving to San Diego by night."

"Where the hell did you hear that?"

"There have been no reports of activity at night. They stayed on the sand at Ocean Beach until daybreak. They have to rest sometime."

"You don't know that!"

"Yes I do!"

"You heard the President. They're going to start bombing the cities. You think the Dragons are going to stay asleep while they do it?"

"I don't care."

"You're not going, Marsha."

"Yes, Jacob, I am! I'd rather die than stay here!"

"My God in heaven. How in hell did I ever hook up with a crazy woman like you?"

"You were lonely, remember?"

Jacob looked around the room, out the window at the gusting wind. "Yeah. I remember," he sighed. He began pulling his luggage from the closet.

* * *

"This is the safest place on Earth," the President's secretary said. "Why do you want to go back to San Diego?"

"My daughter is there. And it's our home."

"Well, we can't keep you against your wishes. The President will think you're deserting him."

"There's nothing more we can do here," Jacob said, speaking for Marsha, who had tears in her eyes again. "If we were with the military, or government, I could see our staying. But we aren't. Tell Mr. Samuels thanks for inviting us, and we wish him well."

* * *

The Malfuscos bought a new purple Honda SUV at a dealership in town. A four-by-four should they need it. They got the car dirt cheap. Next the couple went shopping at the local PX, the secretary forgetting to ask for their cards. The Malfuscos had guilty feelings as they picked from the full shelves. Only yesterday they had walked about town, keeping one eye on the sky as they checked things out. While pubs and restaurants were doing a booming business, most of the retail shops had closed. Grocery stores were empty. Jacob wondered what the people would do once their supplies ran out. The government could only do so much. More than that, he worried about what would happen to him and Marsha when *their* supplies ran out.

They slept fitfully through the afternoon. Once the sun had settled in the west they reviewed the road map one more time. Jacob had grave misgivings about the trip. According to the news the latest estimates put the United States Dragon count at close to two million, thousands having flown in from the islands and up from Central America, completely overrun now except for the northern two-thirds of Mexico. Even with their successes the military was not putting much of a dent in the population. The United States military simply did not have enough manpower to cover the continental forty-eight, and so the combined armed forces concentrated on trying to save the larger inland cities: Cleveland, Chicago, Salt Lake City, Albuquerque, Oklahoma City, Boise, Phoenix, Dallas and the like. Humans all over the globe moved inland, creating chaos in places ill fit to hold them. They made easy meals for the Dragons, and military and police forces around the world were finding that hungry, desperate people were almost impossible to control.

Jacob scrutinized the map. "Let's go with the southern route, through the desert," he said. "Not as many people. We'll go around the bigger cities like Albuquerque. Down 25 to Las Cruces. Spend the day there. That's about eight hours. Then take 10 over to Yuma. Another eight hours. Then maybe three or four hours to San Diego on Highway 8. How does that sound?"

"Like a long time."

Jacob shrugged. "Sorry. Of all the routes it looks the easiest. And safest, if there's anything you can call safe."

"What about gas?"

"We've got double tanks, and extra gas cans. Hopefully they'll be enough."

"And if they're not?"

"I guess we'll hoof it."

"I wish we had weapons," Marsha mused, looking at the map. Despite a rising inner fear she was as determined as ever to go.

"I don't think any weapons we might acquire would do any good against the Dragons. Not from what we've heard, anyway."

"It's not the Dragons I'm worried about, Jake. It's all those hungry people."

* * *

120

Minutes later, with trembling hands, Jacob refolded the map. "You're absolutely sure you want to do this?" he asked one last time.

"Yes, I'm sure! I need to find Tricia, Jake. She said she would meet us in San Diego, at your place, when this was all over."

"It's not over, Marsha. It's never going to be over. This is stupid."

"Damn it, Jacob! I'm not going to argue this with you again. Stay if you want. I have to go! If you had any children of your own you might understand."

"All right. All Right! No need to get angry here," Jacob said. He frowned as his eyes searched the sky for Dragons. Finding none he put the map inside the car on the seat. "And it's not my place, it's *our* place."

"Whatever," Marsha muttered. "Let's go, while I've still got the courage." She walked around the Honda and got in. Jacob followed suit and started the engine. His watch said it was close to seven-thirty. Off to the west rose the lofty peaks of the Rockies, muted now beneath layers of puffy, gray clouds. The streets of the city were empty and dark for the most part, an eerie quiet having settled over them with the onset of twilight. Colorado Springs, like every other still surviving city in the world, had gone underground for the night.

Jacob shivered as a sense of foreboding washed over him. He couldn't believe he was leaving the safest city on the planet, but knew his place was with Marsha. When you were in love, he was finding out, good sense took a back seat to everything else.

Jacob was about to pull out from the curb when a sharp rap came from the roof of the car. Startled, he and Marsha looked out the right side window to find an older person peering back at them. The thin, bearded face with glasses was familiar enough, although they had never met the man. Jacob pushed the proper button and Marsha's window slid down part way.

"Hello," Papalov Darringer said, forcing a smile. He squeezed his forehead, nose and mouth through the opening. Marsha scooted towards Jacob. Darringer was breathing hard, and his face was flushed. In his right hand he clutched a large, bulging suitcase. "Please, forgive me. I was afraid I wasn't going to make it. I'm Dr. Darringer. Papalov Darringer. I saw you both at the meetings?"

"We remember," Marsha said as a strong smell of liquor blew into the car. She fanned the air and moved closer to Jacob.

"Listen, I'll come right to the point," Darringer said. "I was wondering, well, I was wondering if I might hitch a ride with you folks to San Diego? I heard you were leaving. If you're going south I know the roads pretty good, and I have money."

"Hop in," Jacob said after a few seconds. "I don't think your money will be any good, but I'm sure we'll need some help driving."

"Whoa!" Marsha said. "Hold on a minute here."

"Is something wrong?" Darringer asked, his heart sinking. He looked at Marsha.

"Do you have any booze in that suitcase?"

"Well, yes. Some, anyway."

"Good. *Now* you can hop in."

* * *

On the highway between Colorado Springs and Pueblo, a stretch of about forty-five miles, Darringer and the Malfuscos became fast friends. At ease with each other, they found it odd they had never met before, or made acquaintance at The Mountain. The three scientists quickly found they had a lot to talk about.

"I heard your people at Palomar have found three new suns," Jacob said as he drove along, the Honda's headlights piercing the darkness ahead. Except for several long, military convoys moving south, the trio had seen little traffic.

"Yes," Darringer said, sitting beside suitcases and boxes of groceries in the back seat.

"Well, that's nothing new, is it? I mean, you guys are always finding things like that."

"Yes again, but this is different. These suns are traveling together, and right now they're on the outskirts of our solar system, a trillion miles or so outside of Pluto's orbit. Another carrot for the stew."

"But," Jacob protested, "if they're that close, wouldn't you have discovered them long ago?"

Darringer scratched at his beard. "Well, they're not really suns as we know them. About one-twentieth of sol's mass. We believe they've been artificially created, and we believe they have ring worlds around them. Huge ring worlds. So huge they blot out most of the light, another reason we didn't discover them sooner."

"I thought ring worlds were built around planets, not suns," Marsha said, getting in on the conversation.

"These are around suns. We believe this is where the Dragon eggs originated, and the space ships are coming from. The ships are not coming light years to visit us, as many have speculated. They're coming a relatively short celestial distance to harvest their crop. Once that's done, we hope they'll go home. We've calculated the three suns and their worlds will continue to orbit well outside our solar system. There should be minimal gravitational fluctuations here, if any. We're just a fast food stop on the way."

"Incredible," Marsha said. "I knew it was something like that!" Smiling, she took a small sip from a pint of Red Eye that Darringer had given her earlier.

"For Christ's sake," Jacob said. "On the way to where?"

"We have no idea. Current thinking, originated by your wife, has it they travel the galaxy in some great orbit, harvesting worlds for minerals and food as they move about, to keep them going. Unfortunately, this time around, I don't think our visitors are going to like what they find here when they arrive."

"How do you mean?" Jacob asked.

"Well, we're destroying their food crop," Darringer answered. "I don't think they're going to take kindly to that. To be honest, they may want retribution. And mankind will have to pay."

Jacob sighed. "It just doesn't go away, does it?" he said.

"What?" Marsha asked.

"This God damn nightmare," Jacob said. "It never goes away."

Chapter 23
Night of Terror

The three refugees talked for long periods of time as they drove south into the night, pausing infrequently to catch their breath. They talked of family and friends, their time on Earth, their careers. There were short spells along the road where they were even able to forget the peril they were in. Under a spectacular sky, studded with rivets of fire, they watched as the high plains to the east and the mountains to the west rolled peacefully by, lulling them into a false sense of security. Only an occasional car or truck headed north, or another military convoy headed south, broke the stillness of the countryside.

"Those guys are in a hurry," Marsha remarked at one point, after Jacob had pulled to the side of the road to let a convoy pass. Over a hundred vehicles roared by, complete with tanks, artillery, helicopters, armored vehicles, missile launchers and weary looking troops.

"Must be a battle going on somewhere," Papalov said. "That's the biggest convoy I've seen, and I've seen a few."

"What do you think our chances are?" Jacob asked later, outside of Las Vegas, New Mexico.

"Not good," Darringer replied. "Like I said, when they see what we've done here, they'll probably try to eradicate whoever of us are left, like you would ants in your sugar."

"Jesus, Pappy," Jacob said. "You honestly believe they'll take us all out?"

"Well, they won't get us all. There'll always be survivors in a war. But most of us will be gone. Humanity might never recover. They might even harvest us in lieu of the Dragons we've killed. Got to eat, you know."

"Then you don't believe they could be benevolent?" Marsha said. "Take us under their wing? Show us the stars?"

"Well, if our theories are true, they've been harvesting Earth for hundreds of thousands of years, perhaps millions. I think they'll look at us as competition, the way we looked at Indians here in America. I'm sorry to be so negative, but that's the way I see it. Maybe it was their planet to begin with. Maybe they're that old. Maybe they *made* Earth, our whole damn solar system! The possibilities are endless. It boggles your mind."

"You're saying they're God," Marsha said.

"Not quite. But they're close."

"I hope you're wrong," Marsha said.

"So do I."

* * *

Jacob, Marsha and Papalov drove on the outskirts of Santa Fe and Albuquerque in almost complete silence, shocked by what was going on around them. Both cities were packed with refugees, living in shanty towns worse than any the trio had ever seen. Bonfires punctuated the night, and Jacob had to wonder where the fuel was coming from. Roads were clogged and, were it not for National Guardsmen directing traffic, the trio might never have made it through. Military personnel from all branches were kept busy trying to keep order and set up defense lines at the same time. With the help of local police it seemed they were succeeding. Anyone passing through was allowed to keep going, regardless of direction, which made things a whole lot easier than expected for the threesome.

"Designated cities," Jacob said on the freeway skirting Albuquerque. "If I remember right the President designated about twenty-five or so of our larger inland cities west of the Mississippi as sanctuaries."

"And about the same on the east side," Papalov added.

"Some sanctuaries," Marsha added, despairing for the ragged bands of people roaming the two cities in search of food and shelter, some already reduced to begging, others freezing in the cold, early morning air. The adults and children she saw were hollow-eyed, dirty, weary and had an aura of hopelessness about them. Marsha had to wonder how this had ever come about in her beloved Untied States. Surprisingly, in both cities, no one had tried to rob them of their SUV and belongings, something they had feared. Even so, all three were more than happy to get out of Albuquerque and onto the open road again.

"That was scary," Marsha said on leaving the city.

"I don't think we're even close to scary yet," Jacob said, stepping on the gas.

* * *

Around five A.M. Marsha pulled the Honda into a roadside rest stop outside of Organ, a small town situated several miles east of Las Cruces, New Mexico. Unknown to her, east of them lay the White Sands missile range, at present a hotbed of military activity. A hundred searchlights danced over and around the base, looking for the enemy and guiding friendly aircraft to and fro. Marsha cringed as a trio of fighter jets skimmed by overhead, soon to be followed by a dozen or more attack helicopters. The noise was deafening, and the vibrations from the passing aircraft caused the ground, the Honda and all three of its weary passengers to shake uncontrollably for a few seconds.

"I hope it's safe enough here," Marsha whispered to herself once the helos had passed, watching as they disappeared over some low hills to the west. Marsha, disoriented, confused the glow from distant Phoenix as the sun rising in the east. Jacob sat beside her, bleary eyed and still half asleep even though the roar from the jets had almost exploded the car. Papalov sat in back, in worse condition than Jacob. The rest stop was crowded, but not packed as the two cities had been. Marsha figured the people here to be stragglers, the tail lend of those moving on to Albuquerque and Denver.

"It doesn't look like the Dragons have made it this far," Marsha said, loudly this time, loud enough to cause the two men to sit up straight and open their eyes. "Not yet, anyway."

"I wonder what's going on over there?" Jacob said, stifling a yawn. He pointed towards the searchlights flooding White Sands. "Looks like lots of military stuff going in and out."

"People, too," Marsha added, following Jacob's point.

"That's White Sands missile base," Darringer said from the back seat, rubbing his eyes. "I'll tell you, if it were up to me I'd be activating all our missiles and pointing them towards the places those ships will be landing. Blow them to the moon and back. Now wouldn't that be something? Then they'd have no way to transport their cattle. Dragons would rule the Earth."

"In case you hadn't noticed, Pappy," Jacob said, "they already do."

"The problem is, nobody knows where they'll land," Marsha said.

"You told them where," Jacob said.

"That was guessing," Marsha said. "Besides, there are only thirty-six ships, and hundreds of places they could dock. Even if they only hit the pyramids, how many of those still lay buried? Like the one . . . like the one Trish and I discovered."

"Yeah, another damn problem," Jacob said, feeling Marsha's despair, trying to hide his own. "There are too many unknowns in this equation when you think about it. The whole thing eats at your spirit. It pecks holes in you until you bleed to death. I feel like I'm drowning. I'm sick of it!"

"Then don't think about it," Marsha soothed. She leaned over and kissed her husband on the ear. "Just think about getting us home."

Jacob wanted to yell "And then what?" but held his tongue. He knew the only thing keeping his wife sane right now was the thought of one day seeing her daughter again, even though Jacob knew the chances were slim and none of ever doing that. Still, it was a goal, and the only one they had at the moment. The trio was silent for a while, becoming drowsy again, listening to the hum of the Honda's engine that Marsha had left running to keep the car warm. At the very moment she reached out to turn it off two missiles blasted off in the distance, jolting the threesome wide awake. The noise was so deafening the trio had to cover their ears, and the light so bright they turned their heads. When they could see again they caught two missiles arching in the sky, one headed east and one west.

Papalov rubbed tired eyes and watched as the two rockets roared across the sky, spitting fire from their tails.

"The cities," he said, looking off to the west. "They're firing on our cities. They have to be. My God in heaven, I never thought we'd have to resort to that."

"You don't know for sure," Marsha said, straining her eyes.

"Yes. I do."

"They're not nukes, are they?" Marsha asked, her heart pounding. "They wouldn't do that, would they? Not to our own people."

"They're getting desperate," Papalov answered, staring as the east bound missile vanished into a brightening sky. "But I don't think they'll use nuclear weapons. That wouldn't solve anything. Not with the fall out, and all."

"You hope," Jacob said, becoming more and more pessimistic as the hours ticked by.

"We all hope," Marsha said, fighting back tears.

* * *

After a few minutes listening to his wife cry, after reaching out to comfort her and having his hand batted away, Jacob exited the Honda and stretched. He was soon followed by Papalov and a distraught Marsha. Jacob hurried around the car and wrapped his arms around his wife until she stopped crying, consoling her until the last of the tears had been wiped away. Finding the morning cold they donned heavy coats, then grabbed a quick meal of wheat bars and cranberry juice. The trio ate slowly, the silence of the morning broken frequently as more missiles blasted off from the base. Once their meal was done, tarps and sleeping bags came out of the Honda and were tossed beneath a spreading elm, dappled now with brilliant fall colors. They found themselves sharing the rest stop with close to a thousand other people, most trying to sleep, or huddled around campfires to ward off the morning chill. Over coffee, heated on a two-burner Coleman stove, they listened to the gossip.

"They've destroyed the Imperial Valley and Las Vegas," an elderly man said, sipping at a cup of coffee Marsha had offered him. "Yuma, Kingman, Lake Havasu. Ran out of gas east of Phoenix and been walkin' ever since. Most everybody here has been walkin'. No gas nowhere. No food or water, either. They'll probably be in Phoenix by this afternoon. Prescott, Flagstaff and all the rest. Me and my lady are from El Centro. Ran a 7-11 there. So far we been lucky but looks like we'll be runnin' into them Dragons sooner or later. Can't go much farther. Legs is tired and my lady has been feelin' poorly. Don't matter much anyway. No place left to run the way we see it. Lotsa folks on the road back there. They just give up. Waitin' to be saved, I guess. Or die."

The stories from other people were similar. They listened to a young couple from San Diego. The woman cradled a dirty, three-month-old boy in her arms, the man a two-year-old girl, her dress and coat in tatters, her hair matted and uncombed.

"The whole town is gone," the young man, a former carpenter, said. "Some people stayed behind and some got out, but most are dead if what I heard is right. People should have stayed in the city, hidden in the concrete buildings. People running everywhere were like shooting cattle at feed to these things. It was a terrible sight. And the military, they didn't do much. Caught with their pants down, I guess. Just as scared as the rest of us. Scared to bomb the towns for the people, scared to shoot for the people. Should have got them things on the beaches, before they moved inland. Should have done a lot of things but they didn't. Don't have any food for my kids and don't know where to go."

The Malfuscos and Darringer talked to several others before they lay down, exhausted from their long night. They had a hard time sleeping. Helicopters came and went. Jets roared by overhead. The highway became choked with military personnel, some stationed at the rest stop to try and maintain order, for which the trio was thankful.

"Something's going on," Jacob said around noon, when the roar of more missiles being fired woke them all up. "Something big," he added, watching contrails arch east and west.

Marsha sat up and rubbed her eyes. She had given the young couple food and water before dozing off, over the silent disapproval of both Jacob and Papalov. It was something she had to do, even if it meant her own deprivation down the road. Starving children was not an option in her book.

"Wish I had a cold beer," she said, beginning to sweat under a warm, midday sun. She took off her coat and straightened up, then looked at Jacob. "I still don't understand why we can't whip a bunch of dumb animals," she said above the whumpwhumpwhump of helicopters passing over. "With all our military strength you'd think this would be over by now."

"Well, they're not dumb animals," Papalov said, turning on his sleeping bag to face Marsha. "They know enough to stay out of our way, and that's where the problem is. You can't follow them, like a traditional army. Hell, you can't see them! They don't show up on satellite. Most of the time they fly too low for radar. You never know which way they're going, and they cover too much area. You never go head to head on a battlefield, like armies of old. They're more like guerrillas. Hit and run. It's tough. We lost the war in Vietnam because the enemy employed similar tactics. There doesn't seem to be any way to win unless you saturate bomb the areas you think they're in, and how long can you do that before you run out of ammunition? God help any humans left in cities that are under attack. They're getting it from both ends."

"I hope the President understands that," Marsha said.

"I'm sure he does," Papalov said.

Jacob was about to comment when several military transport tucks drove up and parked. Soon the rest stop was surrounded by a hundred or so army reserves, two tanks and several pieces of heavy artillery. An Apache attack helicopter landed in a nearby field and settled in, its rotors kicking up dust and debris. A group of uniformed men and women on one of the trucks began passing out food and water to grateful recipients, including those National Guardsmen that had been there in the first place.

"At least they're trying to look after us," Marsha said as tears formed in her eyes again. "I thought nobody cared."

"Not a bad time to be in the military," Jacob said. He sat up on his sleeping bag and handed Marsha a handkerchief.

"Why do you say that?" Papalov asked. He watched as one of the tanks positioned itself on a small, grassy knoll. The grinding, clanking noises it made were somehow soothing to the people gathered there.

"When push comes to shove they'll be looking after themselves," Jacob answered. "There won't be enough food and supplies for the rest of us."

"Are you always this grim, or is it just me?" Papalov asked.

"He's always this grim," Marsha answered for Jacob. "Lately, anyway."

The trio watched the army set up for a while, then, still tired, lay down and drowsed the afternoon away, more secure now that the military was there. Waking up at five they prepared a small meal of soups and bread, which they shared with the young couple and several others. The military had simply not had enough to go around.

"Good way to lose weight," Jacob said after finishing his soup. No one laughed.

Around seven-thirty, once the sun had set behind the western hills, Jacob, Marsha and Papalov, wondering if they would survive the night, said good-bye to their newfound friends and took to the road. Three pairs of eyes began searching the sky but saw only a smiling three-quarter moon and a million twinkling stars.

"I wonder how they're doing up there?" Papalov said. "Those people on the moon. And those people going to Mars?"

"I'd rather take my chances here," Marsha said, and the two men nodded their agreement.

"Here's hoping that Marsha is right, and they don't fly at night," Jacob said a ways down the road. "But, my question is, if they turn the color of the sky, how would anyone ever know?"

* * *

Shortly after midnight the trio was stopped at a roadblock outside the small town of Benson, Arizona, about fifty miles east of Tucson. Off in the distance, towards Tucson, intermittent, hellish colored explosions pressed against the sky. Smoke billowed, and repetitive, loud "WHUMPS" could be heard coming from the direction of Tucson. A rank, acidic odor filled the air as shock waves followed the explosions, some so strong they shook the SUV. Three already terrified hearts beat faster. Jacob, in the driver's seat, forced himself to remain calm.

"What's up, Officer?" he asked, leaning out the window. The roadblock was manned by two Marines, a young, square jawed second lieutenant and an older, grizzled staff sergeant. Both carried M-16s, needed a shave and wore agitated, nervous expressions. Around their bodies were wrapped bandoleers of ammunition, hand grenades and other utensils of war. The lieutenant leaned close to Jacob and looked inside the car, then backed off a few steps.

"Y'all mind tellin' me what the hell you people are doin' out here in the middle of the desert in the middle of the night? You people stupid or somethin'?"

Marsha leaned across the seat. She smiled her best smile. "We're going home, Colonel," she said. "To San Diego. My daughter lives there."

The lieutenant bent over to get a better look. "Lady," he said, scowling, "y'all are not goin' anywhere but back where you came from. Now turn around and get goin'. Don't y'all be tryin' somethin' stupid here. In case nobody noticed, there's a war goin' on up ahead. There's a whole mess of Dragons in Tucson, and they're meaner than anything you ever dreamed about. You want to get et?"

"But . . ." Marsha protested, at a loss for words at the sudden change in her plans. The sergeant, standing behind the lieutenant, lowered his rifle and pointed it towards Jacob.

"All right," Jacob said, staring down the muzzle. "Okay! No need to get excited here, Sergeant. This wasn't my idea anyway." He put the car in reverse and began backing up. The sergeant, satisfied, slung his rifle over his shoulder.

"Damn it, Jake," Marsha said. "Don't you go and wimp out on me now. Not after we've come this far. You promised me we were going home!"

"I changed my mind."

"Damn you! I didn't! Now pull of the road and get out if you're going to be such a wuss. I'm going home!"

Jacob didn't answer. When the two Marines turned to light a cigarette Jacob slipped the Honda in forward and gunned the engine. Tires screeched and gravel flew. The SUV hit the guard rail going forty on one side and fifty on the other. Splintered wood flew everywhere. Caught by surprise the lieutenant and the sergeant were barely able to jump out of the way before being run over. Regaining his balance first the sergeant whipped the rifle off his shoulder and aimed it at the fleeing Honda.

"No!" the lieutenant shouted, slamming his hand on the rifle barrel and pushing it down. "Let 'em go. If I had a daughter somewhere's right now I'd sure as hell want to go and see if she was still alive."

"But they'll never get through Tucson, sir."

"They'll have a better chance there than your shootin' them here, Sergeant. Besides, we don't know a damn thing about what's goin' on inside the city. Maybe they'll make it and maybe they won't. It's out of our hands."

* * *

"Are they following?" Marsha asked as Jacob kept his foot on the pedal. She peered out the back window along with Papalov, her heart beating three miles a minute.

"I don't see anything," Papalov answered. He took a deep breath. "My oh my," he added after turning to look at Jacob. "I thought for sure that Marine was going to fire at us."

"Must have changed his mind," Jacob said, letting his foot off the gas as the SUV approached 100 MPH. His hands held the steering wheel in a death grip as he began tap-tap-tapping on the brake pedal. He had never driven over 100 in his life, and he didn't want to start now, especially with his SUV shaking so bad. Not that it mattered. As far as he was concerned they were goners anyway. Or would be, once they neared Tucson.

Seconds later Jacob ducked involuntarily when a trio of Apache attack helicopters tore by overhead, headed for Tucson. The roar from their engines and rotor blades drowned out everything else. Jacob's foot slipped off the brake pedal and onto the gas, causing the Honda to swerve onto the shoulder, then back onto the highway. Fighting for control Jacob found the brake pedal again and hit it hard, causing the Honda to swerve back onto the shoulder and spin before finally coming to rest in the middle of the road, facing the direction they had just come from.

"Damn!" Jacob wheezed. "I thought they were going to shoot at *us*!" Jacob reached over and turned the engine off, much to the relief of his passengers. While sitting there, trying to catch their breath, the trio couldn't help but notice that the flashes on the horizon were brighter now, and more frequent. They watched in horror as a half dozen missiles converged on Tucson from the east. Seconds later the city literally exploded. Large pieces of buildings, autos and undescribable things made flaming arcs through the night sky, hurtling outwards into the surrounding desert.

"My god in heaven," Marsha said, holding her hands to her face in disbelief. They began to shake as her face turned the color of blood. "They're destroying Tucson! There are people in there, Jacob. There has to be!"

Jacob, shaken from the events and what he was seeing, could find no words to speak. He and his two companions watched, spellbound, as the city erupted over and over, great balls of fire mushrooming into the sky. All three jumped when what was left of a door and its frame landed not fifty yards from where they were sitting, sending sparks and embers flying everywhere. Marsha became hysterical.

"We'll never get through there!" she screamed, staring at the horizon, watching the horror, feeling the pain, hearing the souls cry out. "I'll never see my daughter again, my home! What's the point here? What's the point of going on? If we do survive there's not going to be anything left. Not if they level all the cities!"

Jacob reached over and grabbed Marsha. He pulled her to him and rocked her in his arms, held on tight to his shaking wife.

"Hold on, baby," he whispered softly. "Hold on."

"Must be a lot of the enemy in the city," Papalov said from the back seat, his voice breaking, trying to change the subject, trying to break Marsha's fear, her torment, his heart gone out to the woman he had met but hours before. He watched as fingers of fire crisscrossed the sky, only to be swallowed up by pillars of smoke. "Samuels said it might be the only way to stop them. Destroying our cities. Apparently he meant it. Those helicopters. I can't imagine how many of our soldiers. Missiles for Pete's sake! I'll bet the police and military have that poor city completely surrounded, ready to shoot anything that tries to get out."

"Ready to help the people, too," Jacob said, trying to console a still sobbing Marsha.

"At least they're not using nuclear weapons," Papalov said, then wished he hadn't.

"Not yet!" Marsha said, pulling herself from Jacob's arms. She sat up and faced Papalov, wiping at tears she didn't know she had left. "No, not yet! What are we going to do now? Can anyone tell me? How in God's name are we going to get to San Diego? It's over! For us and, and everyone," she added. Marsha covered her face with her hands, trying to stop tears that would not stop. Frustrated, Jacob looked out the window, the one facing away from Tucson.

"Now who's being a wuss?" he shouted, angry at having let his wife talk him into this suicide mission.

Papalov leaned forward a put a hand on Marsha's shoulder.

"Listen," he said to both, "I know a place. Kitt Peak. It's a national observatory, not too far from here. It's pretty much a self contained small town of telescopes and other buildings. Maybe seventy or eighty miles southwest of Tucson. It's up about seven thousand feet. Nice and cool and the air is clean. Beautiful this time of year. The peak is a second home to me. I studied there as a graduate student, and I work there off and on, or did. I know some people. They'll take us in."

"If they're alive, Pappy!" Marsha said, lowering her arms. She wiped at her eyes with the back of her hand. "Get real."

"We can get there from here?" Jacob asked, turning to face Papalov.

"Don't see why not. I know the back roads. Or used to, anyway. Did some hunting there when I was young, with some of my fellow students. Out in the desert. Jackrabbits and cottontails. We even hunted rattlesnakes on occasion! We can get a good meal, clean up. Highway 98 is just north of the peak. It will take us to Gila Bend and back to highway 8. We can get to San Diego from there, avoiding Tucson altogether."

"Pappy, you're a lifesaver," Jacob said. He looked at Marsha, who had her handkerchief out.

"How does that sound, sweetheart? We'll get a good day's rest, and be on the road again tomorrow evening."

Marsha sniffed and blew her nose and nodded her head. "All right," she said, brightening at the prospect. "That sounds good."

"Then it's settled," Jacob said. "Would you like to drive?" he asked, looking to Papalov.

* * *

Three hours later, after navigating some rough back roads and getting lost twice, the trio found themselves winding up a steep, two-lane mountain road. The time was close to five A.M., and the weary travelers could see a soft glow beginning to light the eastern horizon behind them. As beautiful as the scenery was, and thankful for their safety, the morning was dampened by the sight of Tucson burning to the northwest. Farther north they could see an ominous orange glow lighting the horizon.

"Must be Phoenix," Papalov said, despondent. "They must have bombed her last night, too. Probably a whole line of cities along this latitude, if the Dragons are moving according to how we think they're moving. Salt Lake, Pocatelo in Idaho, Butte and Great Falls in Montana. Who knows what's happening in the east, and how far the Dragons are inland there?"

"Or how far north in Mexico," Jacob said, peering out the side window towards Phoenix, his nose pressed against the window.

Marsha, numb from the trip and the thought of American cities being destroyed, fought back further depression. She loved her husband dearly, but right now the only thing keeping her mind on track was the thought of seeing her daughter again. She knew Tricia was still alive. She just knew it.

"Do you think we can stop them?" Jacob asked as Papalov rounded a sharp curve a little too fast for him. Miles ahead they caught a glimpse of Kitt Peak, bathed now in glittering sunlight. Jacob couldn't count the number of small, dome shaped observatories he saw, nestled among high desert shrubs and trees. The effect was stunning and, if it were not for the situation, Jacob would have thought the peak incredibly beautiful.

"I do, eventually," Papalov answered, wishing he were coming home under different circumstances. It had been a long time since his last visit, and he dearly loved the mountain. A wave of memories washed through his mind, clear back to when he was a young, fresh and eager graduate student. Now, forty-two years later, life had taken its toll. The wife he had met here, who had died of liver cancer almost a decade ago. The two children he never saw, the five grandchildren he would probably never see again. His bad back, the bladder problem. Still, like everyone else, he continued on, betting on tomorrow. Only now tomorrow loomed an impossible nightmare and, like Marsha, he continued on for love of family, and the outside hope he might one day see them again.

"Yes, I think we will," he continued. "Here in the States, anyway. I don't know about the rest of the world. What happens when the Dragons overrun the other nations? If we survive, then what's to keep them from coming here and finishing us off? Even so, over time, I think we might win. But what's the point? Even if we defeat them, the space ships will follow up. Speaking of which, maybe up here at Kitt we can get an update. We're definitely not getting anything on the radio."

"A lot of static," Jacob said, his nose still pressed against the window.

"Plenty of that, for sure."

Papalov was winding around a hairpin curve when he spotted the school bus lying at an angle in a dry stream bed. The side of the vehicle nearest the road was ripped open.

"What in the world?" Papalov muttered as he pulled onto a small turn out. Leaving the engine on he jumped from the SUV and was quickly followed by Jacob. Marsha stayed inside, her hands to her face again.

"Must have rolled," Jacob said, working his way ahead of the elderly Papalov and through some heavy brush to the crash site.

"Don't think so," Papalov said. "The top is still intact."

Twenty yards later Jacob and Paplov found themselves at the bottom of a steep, sandy slope where the bus had come to rest against some stunted pine trees. Peering through the large gap in the side of the bus the two men saw no bodies, but there was blood. Blood on the seats, blood on the walls, blood everywhere.

"My god," Jacob said, suddenly on the alert. "They've been here! What else could have ripped the side out like that?"

"I don't know," Papalov said, his heart racing. He looked around, scrutinizing every inch of the sky and terrain. "But I can take a guess. We need to get out of here, and now. It's getting daylight, and those things could be sizing us up."

"Well, that's a comforting thought," Jacob said, fighting to stay calm. "But we can't just leave, can we? I mean, maybe some of the children escaped. We have to rescue them."

"You're not thinking straight here," Papalov countered. "We need to leave." He grabbed Jacob's arm and began pulling him towards the Honda. Jacob pulled free and was about to go around the bus when he heard a loud rustling from farther down the slope.

"Damn," he said under his breath. Jacob turned and made a bee line back up the hill, Papalov close behind.

* * *

When nothing followed the trio breathed easier, but not much. Their fear was forgotten for a moment, however, when they neared the top of Kitt Peak. All around them stretched a panorama of breathtaking mountains rising from an endless, flat desert. The sky was clear, the air fresh, cool and invigorating, but their euphoria was short lived. Around the next corner a scene of unbelievable devastation greeted them. Within the large complex that comprised the Peak several observatories lay crushed, while others had their sides torn out. Most of the buildings were smoldering, with fires still burning here and there. Smoke billowed and danced high into the sky before being caught in a stiff wind and hurried off on a southwesterly course. A large, rectangular building was completely flattened, as if in the path of a hurricane. Autos, trucks and trailers lay on their sides, or upside down. A handful looked as if they had been torched. Trees and shrubs lay uprooted and burned. Nothing moved.

"My god," Jacob said, driving slowly down a road between several observatories. "Those things must be huge by now to do something like this."

"Obviously!" Papalov said, agitated. "Look, get in the game, would you? We can gawk later, Jacob. Right now we need to find a spot to hide, to spend the day. And quick! They may still be here."

"You don't know that," Marsha said, finding her voice after a lengthy silence. The demolished bus had sent her imagination into overtime, and she was finding it hard to function.

"And I don't want to know, either," Papalov countered, then: "Jacob! Up there! On the ridge? Do you see it?"

"What, for Christ's sake?" Jacob asked, his heart almost stopping. "Where?"

"The observatory! Take a right here. Follow the road."

"What do you see?"

"I don't see anything! And I don't want anything to see us. Now hurry!"

Caught up in Papalov's anxiety, Jacob gunned the SUV. He rounded several curves too fast, almost flipping the Honda on one of them. Finally they reached the top of the hill and Jacob turned into a small parking lot, skidding to a stop but a foot or two from a steep embankment. Except for one burned out pickup the lot was empty.

"Get out!" Papalov barked, putting himself in charge. "Around the side. Into the building! There's a door there. I think I saw something move in those trees down in the canyon. Something big."

"What?" Jacob said. He opened the door and looked around. "What the hell did you see?" he asked as he got out, his heart pounding. Not getting an answer, Jacob hurried around to help a petrified Marsha.

"Never mind!" Papalov shouted, leaving the Honda. A high pitched, screeching filled the air. Jacob heard an unfamiliar sound, one he discerned as wings beating against air. Huge wings. Running now, Papalov began pushing the Malfuscos ahead of him. "Keep moving!"

Jacob looked over his shoulder in time to see an impossibly large creature bearing down on them. The alien monster was a composite of every picture of every Dragon he had ever laid eyes on. A combination of dinosaur and bird, terrible and deadly, yet at the same time beautiful and magnificent. The Dragon screeched again, a high pitched, grating sound. Jacob put one of his arms behind his back as he grabbed Marsha's hand and began pulling her.

"Run, baby!"

Papalov stumbled. With a last effort he pushed Jacob and Marsha towards the door. Falling face forward Papalov hit and rolled. He pulled a pistol from his belt and began firing towards the approaching shadow. Jacob and Marsha ran up the observatory steps to the door and, finding it locked, pressed themselves up against it, trying to flatten themselves out. They watched in horror as the huge, iridescent, rainbow colored beast caught Papalov in its claws, turned, climbed high into the air and then, gliding in a graceful arc, carried the struggling astronomer deep into the canyon. Marsha began screaming, a terrified, incomprehensible scream, a scream straight from hell.

Jacob unglued himself from the wall and ran down the steps after Papalov's pistol. He retrieved it, ran back up the steps and blew the lock off the door. He grabbed Marsha, still screaming, and dragged her inside. Slamming the door Jacob looked around at the shattered ceiling, the burned out interior, and, deciding on a downward route, led his wife along winding steps into a basement of sorts. There the duo huddled for hours, wrapped in each other's arms, too terrified to move.

Chapter 24
Perilous Journey

Despite their ordeal the Malfuscos fell asleep, in each other's arms, shortly after noon. They slept the sleep of the totally exhausted, deep and dreamless, their bodies gathering strength for whatever lay ahead. When they awakened, around seven that evening, the duo crept back up the basement steps to the main floor. Still stunned by the loss of their newly found friend, Jacob opened the door a crack and peered out. Seconds later he opened it farther, then stepped back into the relative safety of the building.

"I'm sorry, Jake," Marsha said, standing beside her husband and taking his hand. "I'm so dense. I really didn't believe all this was happening until we lost Pappy. And I'm responsible." She let go of Jacob's hand and stepped out onto the small, concrete porch just outside the door. Looking northeast, through the encroaching darkness, she could still see distant Tucson. What was left of the city was now a small, blazing half-sun, shrouded beneath thick layers of smoke. Farther north, barely discernible through a dense haze that blanketed the desert floor, another half-sun glowed. "I didn't believe it at all. I was in denial. I thought that we would have won by now, that it would all be over."

"Me too," Jacob said, coming out to stand by Marsha. "And you're not responsible for his death. He asked us if he could come along, remember? He knew the danger." Jacob scanned the skies and the immediate area before staring over her shoulder at the canyon below. "Pappy was a good man," he reflected. "From what we knew of him, anyway."

"He hardly knew us. Why didn't he try to save himself?"

"Altruism, honey. One human's love for another. It's unexplainable, but I can tell you this. If we're ever to get through this thing, then humanity is going to need all the altruism it can muster. That, and a lot of other things, like learning to love one another again. Anyway, you think you're ready to move on?"

"I guess so," Marsha answered. She searched the sky and the canyons for Dragons. "Are you sure they don't come out at night?" she asked, her heart filled with dread.

"You said that, I didn't. And no, I'm not sure of anything, sweetheart, except that we can't stay here."

"We have nothing much left to eat, and our water's about gone. What about gas?" Marsha fretted.

"They must have a cafeteria up here, and I think Pappy said they have a small general store. We'll have to find them. Hopefully there'll be some things left."

"And the gas?"

"We'll siphon some if there's no station. But there has to be, for the maintenance trucks if nothing else. I thought ahead for once, and brought a hose. And we have the cans."

Taking deep breaths they ran to the car. It didn't take long to find the general store. Scrounging around inside the crushed building, using flashlights they'd brought along, the Malfuscos found food and water. Plenty of it. Apparently, despite the broken windows and caved in ceiling, the Dragons had been unable to work themselves inside. There was blood by the entrance, however, and on several of the overturned cars in the parking lot.

"Why didn't they leave?" Marsha asked, spraying her flashlight around. She picked over canned goods scattered on the floor beneath toppled shelves.

"Where could they go? Pappy said most of his people stayed on at Palomar. This mountain looks like about as safe a place as any, tucked way out here in the middle of nowhere. Why leave? Maybe they were like us, thinking the Dragons would never get this far, thinking that it would all be over by now. More to the point, they probably figured the Dragons wouldn't bother with such a remote outpost. That would be my guess."

"I suppose no place is safe," Marsha said. She picked up a couple of cans of pork 'n beans, put them in her carrying basket.

Worried and distraught the Malfuscos went about their tasks, one eye on what they were doing and one eye on the world outside. Marsha was on her way to the crumpled entrance, her baskets loaded down, when there was a loud crash. The ceiling moved. She saw movement from the corner of her eye. Scared witless she dropped her baskets, along with her flashlight, and turned into a darkened room. Something grabbed her leg. Marsha screamed. Something grabbed her about the waist. Finding it hard to breathe, and on the verge of blacking out, Marsha looked down in time to see the outline of a chubby, three-year-old girl holding onto her leg for dear life. Clutching her around the waist was another young girl, this one an eight-year-old blonde; slim, blue eyed and beautiful despite her matted and torn hair. Marsha couldn't believe her eyes. Regaining her senses almost instantly she dropped to her knees and wrapped her arms around the children. The girls hugged her so tight, about the neck now, that Marsha was afraid they might cut her circulation off.

"Jacob!" she managed to yell, her voice all but strangled. "Come here! We've got company!"

* * *

After securing enough gas to get them to San Diego the Malfuscos, along with Mindy and Megan Sheldon, made their way down the mountain. Overhead scattered clouds raced beneath a bright moon, causing shadows to dance across the desert floor. Off in the distance Tucson and Phoenix still burned. The Malfuscos tried not to look.

In the back seat, Mindy Sheldon, the older of the two girls, talked rapidly, her eyes wide and excited as she recalled the events of the last few days. Megan, half asleep, cuddled against Marsha in the front seat. Marsha had done a good job of cleaning and consoling the two terrified children. They almost looked human. She adjusted Megan and stroked the little girl's hair as she and Jacob listened.

"We never saw them coming," Mindy was saying. "Not until too late, anyway. There was a whole bunch of them, flying in what Daddy said was a 'V' formation? You know, like the ducks you see in the pictures do? Some of the people had already left for Tucson. My daddy and mommy and some of their friends wanted to stay, saying it would be safer here. But it wasn't. Some of the men had guns but I guess they couldn't shoot very well. They didn't do any good. The big birds came in and started breaking everything. Fire came out of their mouths. People ran and tried to hide but they were too late. My mommy, she hid us in the closet, where they keep the cleaning stuff. She said not to come out until she came back, but she never did. Have you seen her? Have you seen my mommy and daddy?"

Marsha turned around. Reaching back she brushed Mindy's hair with her hand.

"No dear, I haven't. But I betcha they're down the mountain, with some of the other folks."

"But why did they leave me and my sister behind?"

"They must have thought you would be safer there. I'm sure they intended to come back and get you. Me and Jake, here, we just beat them to it."

"They're dead, aren't they? Those big, horrible birds ate them, didn't they?"

"I don't know, baby," Marsha consoled. "I really don't. We'll have to keep looking for them, the way we did on top the mountain. The way I . . . the way I'm looking for my daughter. We left them notes and directions. Maybe they'll find us in San Diego. We just have to keep hoping."

* * *

"I wonder if they did any good?" Jacob said after a while, after they had made it to the bottom of Kitt Peak without incident. He turned left on a deserted Highway 85 and headed northwest. He and Marsha couldn't help but see the glow from the fires still burning off in the distance. Heavy smoke drifted through the numerous valleys, winding its way between the hills and mountain ranges. "Diminished their numbers in any significant quantities, I mean."

"I'm sure they killed quite a few," Marsha said, turning to look at a now sleeping Mindy, the young girl's head propped up against sleeping bags, pillows and blankets in the back seat. She adjusted the snoring Megan once again, continuing to stroke her hair. "These poor kids, they probably got less sleep than you and I over the last few days."

"What are you going to do with them?" Jacob asked, keeping his eyes on the road.

"What do you mean?"

"Well, what?"

"Well, keep them, silly. What else? At least until this is all over with. Why? What do *you* want to do with them?"

"Nothing," Jacob said, sneaking a look at the girls. He had always wanted children. "Just thought I'd ask."

They drove through many smaller cities on their way to San Diego; Ajo, Gila Bend and Dateland in Arizona. Winterhaven and Alpine in California, among others. Once proud and beautiful cities reduced to rubble. Cars lay overturned, windows smashed, homes and business buildings destroyed and burning. Nothing moved except for the random fires and smoke. The larger cities, Yuma, El Centro and El Cajon, were the same. Bleak, devastated war zones, from the smallest to the largest.

It was in Yuma that things changed. A dozen or so hungry and desperate refugees had set up a makeshift roadblock on the highway. Shots were fired by hollow eyed and blood-stained men running onto the highway. Jacob rammed the roadblock, almost flipping the SUV as it flew over boulders and debris, managing to get away. Farther along the road a dirty woman with a baby in her arms tried to wave them down by stepping in front of the speeding Honda. Jacob barely missed her and ended up bouncing the Honda off the guard rail at a high rate of speed, almost rolling over again. Luckily the SUV sustained no major debilitating damage through the ordeals. The mental anguish afforded his passengers was another matter altogether. It took Jacob, parked on a deserted road off the highway, almost half an hour to calm the girls down.

"We'll need to be more careful, is all," Jacob said, catching his breath. "We're probably going to be running into more of this as time goes on."

"That's real optimistic," Marsha said, the color returning to her face.

"It's not optimistic, it's realistic, and we'd better get used to it," Jacob said, worried about the road ahead. "And there's nothing positive out there. The world we've known is coming to an end, Marsha, and we've either got to adjust, or perish."

"Well, listen to you. Thanks, Jake. I never would have know things were getting worse if you hadn't told me."

Not up to an argument, Jacob grunted and started the engine.

* * *

Around four A.M. Jacob topped a rise on Highway 8 and headed downhill towards Mission Hills. Only twenty minutes or so from home now, he and Marsha let out a sigh of relief. Off to their left and right the outline of broken homes and buildings could be seen in the early morning darkness. Again there were no lights, and nothing could be seen on the move. Unlike the other cities they had passed through, however, there were no fires along the highway, or anywhere else that they could see. The taller buildings along the freeway, some thirty stories or more, loomed like ghostly sentinels against the sky. Marsha stared out the window as Jacob sped along the highway, trying to make it home before sunrise. "Doesn't look too bad," Jacob said at one point. "No fires, or anything."

"The Dragons weren't mature enough to light fires," Marsha said. "It doesn't matter," she added, surveying the ruins. "They never had a chance anyway." Tears she didn't know she had came to her eyes again. "They had no warning. They got up Saturday morning to go to work or play and found

Dragons on their doorsteps."

"Don't you get tired of crying all the time?" Jacob said, not only weary from the trip, but worried about what they were going to do now that they had reached their destination.

"You want me to be happy with millions of people dead, Jake? I don't see you laughing all the time."

"Jesus. Forget it," Jacob said. "I didn't mean it that way."

"Which way did you mean it, Mr. hard guy?"

"Never mind."

"I wonder if anyone got out?" Marsha said, changing the subject.

"We did," Jacob said. He turned the SUV onto a sharply rising off ramp, towards a bridge spanning Highway 8 that headed north and south. Jacob looped a loop and veered south.

"But we knew about this before anyone else. And the military came and got us not four hours after we had returned home. Remember? While we were packing. They flew us the hell out of here!"

"Word travels fast, baby. I'm sure most of the people got out," Jacob lied, trying to bolster Marsha's spirits. And his own, for that matter. What would happen to his wife when they came up empty handed searching for her daughter?

"I hope so," Marsha said. She wiped at her tears. "Two million people are a lot of Dragon food."

When Jacob turned off the freeway onto University Avenue, however, his and Marsha's worst fears were realized. Everywhere they looked cars, trucks and busses were overturned, homes and businesses destroyed. Whole blocks were burned out cinders, some structures smoldering from earlier fires. The only thing that moved was a skinny gray cat that ran across the road in front of them, startling the duo.

"It looks as if the fires are out," Jacob said later, gawking as he maneuvered the SUV around a corner.

"Jacob, would you get us home? It's getting light out!"

Jacob was forced make a few detours around blocked roads but finally made it to Georgia Street. All about houses and apartment buildings were in ruins. Tall palms and other trees lay broken and scorched. Shrubs were smashed and uprooted. Miraculously, Jacob's house lay relatively untouched, as were many others up and down his street.

"No one was home here," Marsha surmised, surveying her block. She scanned the skies for movement as Jacob pulled the Honda up to the curb.

Off to the east a faint, orange glow brightened the morning. A cool breeze, smelling of smoke and other things foul, hurried down the street. Off to the south, towards what was left of Balboa Park and a mile or so away, a large shape bore down on them, gliding smoothly, riding the early morning currents. Wings flapped.

"Christ in heaven," Jacob muttered, noticing the Dragon as he made ready to exit the car. Jumping from the SUV he ran around to Marsha's side, which was nearest the curb. "It's coming after *us!*" he shouted, almost running over Marsha as she exited the Honda, Megan still asleep in her arms.

"Get in the house!" he yelled, jerking the door on Mindy's side of the SUV open. Reaching in he grabbed the slowly awakening girl and yanked her from the car. Jacob scooped her up then ran towards the front door, a scant distance of fifteen feet from the curb. The creature screeched, sending waves of terror through Jacob and his wife. Marsha, juggling Megan, fumbled with her keys and dropped them. Overhead the huge creature screeched again and veered, homing in, its underbelly glowing with the first light of dawn. Huge talons barely missed as Jacob knocked everyone to the ground and then fell on top. Once the shadow was past Jacob rolled off the girls and stood up, pulling them off the ground. Mindy began to cry, soon to be followed by little Megan, who always cried whenever her big sister did. Marsha picked up the keys but continued to fumble with the lock. Jacob cursed, having left his keys in the Honda.

"Move it!" Jacob yelled as the Dragon began a long turn, wings beating hard against the air. Marsha continued to fumble. Jacob, exasperated, grabbed at the keys only to have them fall again. The Dragon made a lazy arc in the sky and then, turning, skimmed several tall buildings and homed in on the terrified humans.

"Around back! Hurry!" Jacob yelled, grasping at straws. The Dragon, a giant against the sky, grazed the top of a burned out apartment building and swooped down. Huge wings turned against the wind and broke its descent as immense talons thrust forward to snatch its prey. The foursome was in panic when the front door flew open. Arturo Ramirez, Tricia's Hispanic husband, took one step forward and grabbed the children, pulling them inside. Jacob shoved Marsha ahead of him and followed behind.

"Down! Into the basement!" Arturo shouted, Mindy in one arm and Megan in the other.

The Malfuscos needed no prodding. They had barely made it through the kitchen when the Dragon crashed into the house, smashing in the front. With a loud groan the roof on the two-story home buckled inwards as the fireplace collapsed. Bricks exploded in all directions, falling like rain. Broken glass, splintered wood, plaster and other debris exploded inward, following Jacob and the others downstairs and into the basement. Beams snapped as the old Victorian style house fell in on itself, flattening the second floor onto the first. Timbers groaned as more glass shattered. Jacob grabbed Mindy and rolled to the floor, trying to protect her from falling debris. Marsha screamed, terrified once again. The basement roof moaned and began to sag. Heavy footprints could be heard from above, followed by the tearing of wood and a high pitched, angry screeching. Plaster dust billowed down the steps.

"The son-of-a-bitch sounds hungry!" Jacob said as he shielded Mindy.

"He is trying to get in on us!" Arturo yelled above the din. "Pray that he does not decide to use fire!"

"It's a little late for prayer, Art!" Jacob said as he handed Mindy to Marsha, now kneeling with her hands over her head. Part of the basement roof gave way, showering everyone below with splintered wood and more plaster and dust. Furniture and other household items crashed to the floor. The air became filled with a fine white powder, making it difficult to breathe, and even harder to see. Jacob got to his knees and began crawling over debris towards the steps.

"Where are you going?" Marsha screamed.

"To get my gun!" Jacob yelled as a door opened suddenly to his left.

"In here!" a voice commanded from inside the room. Jacob turned to see his daughter-in-law, Tricia, staring back at him. "It's safer in here. The walls are stronger!" Jacob smiled in recognition, but continued on, determined to get where he was going.

"See ya when I get back, little one," was all he said after reaching over and patting her on the arm.

"Tricia?" Marsha whirled from where she had been kneeling. She couldn't believe her eyes. "Is that really you, love? How did you . . . ?"

"Not now, Mom!" Tricia barked, cutting her off. "Get in here! We can talk later."

Overhead one of the main beams groaned and cracked as the Dragon continued to tear at the house. More plaster fell, then the right side of the hallway began to give. Arturo grabbed Mindy and her sister and passed them through to Tricia. Then he grabbed Marsha beneath the arms and did the same. Above them the ripping and screeching continued.

"Sucker's having a fit," Jacob muttered to himself as he reached the bottom of the stairs and a cabinet beneath them. Jacob stood up, opened the cabinet door and retrieved a vintage, double barreled shotgun, thankful that it was still there. He pulled a box of shells from the only shelf, loaded the gun and was about to start up the stairs when Arturo grabbed him from behind.

"You crazy, man?" Arturo yelled. "There is nothing you can do up there with that little gun. I know. We already tried! Now come and get in the room with us before it is too late."

"But . . ."

"No! No buts!" Arturo commanded and, before Jacob could make a move, the tall, handsome Ramirez had jerked the shotgun from his hands and was running back down the hallway. Jacob took one step up the damaged stairwell and, listening to the havoc going on above, decided to follow Arturo. Before he could make it to Tricia's room shots rang out. Heavy shots, deer rifles or better. The roof groaned, a beam snapped with a loud "CRACK!" and the overhead began to buckle once again. Jacob had no sooner reached the door when Tricia pulled him through. Jacob was greeted by his old, dark wine cellar, a small room, empty now, that was walled in on three sides by mossy, concrete blocks and the other by sloping, damp dirt. A strong, musty odor pervaded the cold, windowless room. Mindy was holding a flashlight and shining it through the doorway. As soon as Jacob was inside Tricia shut the door and turned to face the others. Jacob noticed several of the overhead crossbeams had been shored up with four-by-fours, probably in anticipation of the event that was now occurring. Everyone stared at the ceiling as more shots rang out, jerking with each report. The Dragon screeched, the thrashing stopped and the roof gave a little before springing back up.

"Who's shooting?" Jacob asked as his eyes adjusted to the dim light. Tricia took the flashlight from the wide-eyed Mindy as Arturo opened the door a crack. Marsha held onto a jabbering Megan, the little girl oblivious as to what was going on around her.

"We have a few neighbors up and down the street," Arturo answered, peering through the crack. He cocked an ear towards the ceiling, straining to hear. "They have rifles. It is enough to scare the Dragons away sometimes, but, unless it is a lucky shot, no damage is done. And the Dragons get braver as the hours pass by."

"Is he gone?" Marsha asked, trying to control the rambunctious Megan. Arturo nodded. "I believe so."

Marsha let the girl go. Megan promptly headed for the dirt and began playing in it. "We were unaware Dragons were still in the city," she said, unable to relax.

"Maybe a dozen or so," Tricia said. She smiled at her mother for the first time since seeing her, a weary, tired smile that was quickly gone. "They have nests, or lairs, or whatever it is you want to call them. Over in the park. They seem to like it there, with all the big trees and grass and such. They stay there at night and fly downtown during the day, perching on top of the taller buildings. Looking for food, I guess. Human food. I think we're all that's left. One of them perches on the senior apartments up the street from us from time to time. Apparently they can see for miles. You were lucky you weren't seen sooner. We don't dare go outside anymore. Not during the day, anyway."

"He is gone," Arturo said confidently, still peering out the door. He opened it wider, scrutinized the ceiling. All was silent except for the occasional creaking of the walls and beams as they adjusted to their new weight distributions.

Tricia took in a deep breath and looked at her mother, the thought that they were both alive, and together, starting to sink in. Too tired to stand she crawled the short distance to Marsha and put her arms around her neck, squeezing hard. Marsha hugged her back as the others looked on.

"Dear God, Mom, I thought you were dead," a tearful Tricia said, holding onto her mother for all she was worth. "I don't believe you're here." Megan, watching the two older women, followed suit and began to cry. Jacob shook his head and scooped her up.

"Me too," Marsha said, tears coming again, but happy tears this time, tears of joy and relief. "I thought I would never see you again. God, but you look good!"

"Not that good, Mom," Tricia laughed, then squeezed even tighter. "You always were a good liar."

After several minutes, after the two finally let go of each other and dried their eyes, the group traded stories. Jacob and Marsha, with help from Mindy, told of their harrowing journey from Colorado Springs, then it was Tricia's and Arturo's turn.

"It didn't take long for Santa Monica to be overrun," Tricia said. "Once we figured out what was going on, Art and I decided to stay. Not much choice, really. We hid in a basement there, along with others. When we came out three days later things were a mess. Like here, only worse. The whole city was in ruins, like after a major earthquake. Surprisingly, there weren't a lot of us around. Most everybody fled, I guess. Or tried to. Anyway, after that, we packed up and headed south. On the back roads. At night, like you guys did. We were hoping to find you."

"Yeah," Arturo interrupted. "We had no idea you had gone to Colorado. Pretty fancy company."

"More scared than fancy, I think," Jacob said.

"When we got here," Tricia continued, looking at Jacob, "it was too late to leave. Where could we go? Art brought his broadband radio. We pick up stations from time to time, but there are fewer of them with each passing day. Some of them told of the Dragons moving inland. We thought it might be safe after that, after the Dragons moved on."

"It doesn't seem very safe to me," Marsha said.

"Unfortunately, as you now know, they didn't all move on," Tricia said.

"You cannot travel around in daylight," Arturo said. "This one, he must have seen you coming down Georgia. They have even started hunting at night, something they did not do the first days."

"They're getting hungrier," Tricia said. She moved away from Marsha and sat beside Arturo, took his hand in hers. "With all the people dead or gone east, and all the livestock and dogs eaten."

"Hungry enough to tear this house apart," Jacob said.

Arturo grimaced and shook his head. "That is nothing new, my friend. They have been doing that all along. I am sure they can smell us, like a cat can smell a rat."

"I guess it's just going to be a case of who starves first," Marsha said.

Chapter 25
Moles

They talked awhile, in the dark and the damp, getting reacquainted. Then Arturo changed the subject.

"We should have food enough to last for a while. When we came out of the basement we found groceries left in the stores and, as Tricia has told you, not too many people left to get them. We took what we could bring, and there was a lot when we got here."

"That's my old stuff," Jacob said. "It's been down here awhile. Had it stored for earthquakes. Never thought I'd have to use it under these circumstances. Speaking of which, you guys were pretty brave to travel all this way, you know? Awful risky."

"And you, too," Arturo countered. "But Tricia wanted to see her mother, and so here we are. It has worked out all right."

"For us, anyway," Jacob said.

"What about utilities?" Marsha asked.

"The water's gone," Tricia answered. "Electricity too. We've stocked up as best we could. Got some of the large bottles from neighborhood houses, and gallon jugs from the stores. We'll have to ration. Until it starts raining, anyway. We've stockpiled trash cans and such for when it does."

"Sometimes it doesn't rain here," Jacob said. "Or very little when it does."

"We know that, Jake," Marsha said. "Lighten up."

The group discussed things for a while, watching the air clear as they made plans for the near future. After an hour or so, when the damp and dirty room became too claustrophobic, Arturo ventured out. He and Jacob surveyed the damage, then went outside along with Tricia. Lighting a small oil lamp Marsha stayed in the basement with the children and began cleaning up.

Sneaking around outside Jacob and Arturo took a look at things while Tricia, holding the shotgun, kept an eye out for Dragons. Jacob packed Papalov's .45. They found the north facing wall partially intact, the wall with what was left of the fireplace, but everything else lay crumpled and flat. Overhead clouds were moving in, trying to block a blood red sun. A stout northwesterly pushed the clouds along, clearing the area of a week's stale soot and smoke. Riding the winds was the sweet smell of rain.

"Lucky for us the basement ceiling held," Arturo said. He took a deep breath of the freshening air and looked around. "We will have to cover this with some kind of tarp, to keep out the rain, if we want to stay here. But how are we going to do that?"

"What about next door?" Jacob asked, glancing north to another two story home that bordered his. There was no damage that he could see. He searched the sky as he talked. "Is anyone living there?"

"No," Arturo said, his eyes following Jacob's. "A much better idea than mine, Jacob. Now we had better get back inside before we are seen here."

Jacob paused a second and glanced around the neighborhood he had grown to love. He looked at the rows of destroyed houses down the street, several up the block and at the severely damaged and burned out apartment buildings across the way. The overturned cars and splintered trees. On the sidewalk across the street he could make out what he thought to be blotches of dried blood. Large blotches. What had happened to his neighbors? Their children? The ones he knew well, and the ones he didn't? Old Mr. and Mrs. Wainright and their four poodles? Were they alive? Were they dead? What about his colleagues at State? Would he ever see them again?

Jacob became angry as a wave of depression washed over him.

"What difference does it make if we're seen or not?" he said. "What God damn difference does it make? If the Dragons don't get us we'll starve to death sooner or later. There's no world left anymore Art, Tricia. There's no food to hunt. Have you two thought about that? Do you have any idea of what's going on? Look at my house. Look at my street! It's the same all over, and it's only going to get worse. So what's the point? Who wants to live in a world like this?"

"Yes, we have some idea of what is going on," Arturo answered after a few seconds, after he had scrutinized the sky and the street corners and the tops of buildings. He stared Jacob in the eye. "When the Dragons are gone, Mr. Jacob, and they *will* be gone someday, then we will start over. Those of us who are strong will start over. We are human beings, and that is what human beings do when things like this happen. We will cry for loved ones and feel sorry for ourselves for a while and then we will start again. That is what Tricia and I and the little ones are going to do. We are young, you are old. You can do what you want. As for us, we are going back to the basement and begin moving things before it begins to rain."

"I'm not that old, smart guy," Jacob said.

"Then quit crying and give us a hand."

Miffed, Jacob followed Arturo and Tricia back inside. He told them about the alien suns and their ships. Jacob hadn't wanted to tell them this way but he needed to get even. The stunned looks that crossed Tricia's and Arturo's faces made him wish he'd kept his mouth shut.

* * *

Later, over a late afternoon meal of canned peas, stale bread and Spam, the group discussed their options in the basement of their new home, built almost identically to Jacob's. They sat, tired and weary, while the rains that had begun but an hour earlier increased in their intensity. Where Jacob's basement had been converted into a series of smaller rooms, their new home was a single, large area. There was a low ceiling, supported by several massive wooden beams. Concrete block walls and round, steel posts supported the beams. Jacob and the others had to admit they liked the roominess. Beds and furniture had been set up, mostly from upstairs, and the girls had done a small amount of decorating. A two-burner Coleman stove burned on top of a makeshift counter, doing its best to try and dry out the damp cellar. Towards the center of the room, between two armchairs and on top of a wooden box, an oil lamp burned cheerfully.

"It's amazing," Tricia, said, listening to the pitter-patter of raindrops outside. She sat, along with Arturo, around an oak table that had seen better days, salvaged from the upstairs dining room. Off in a corner baby Megan played happily with some blocks and other toys Marsha had given her, courtesy of the previous tenants. "Despite all that's going on I still love the rain, the sound of it. At least that's still the same."

"Filling the buckets, too," Arturo said.

"Maybe it will rain enough to put the last of the fires out," Jacob said through a mouthful of peas, "and we can breathe again."

"Jacob! Enjoy the moment!" Marsha chastised from where she sat with Mindy, a hot cup of tea in her hand. "Quit being so grumpy. Life goes on."

"For how long?"

"Oh, Jesus!"

"Maybe it will melt the Dragons," Mindy said, with her own little cup of tea, not quite as hot as Marsha's. She and Marsha sat in front of a single barred basement window. Mindy looked out through the streaking rain, a wistful look on her face. "And then Megan and I can go home and be with

Mommy and Daddy."

"Wouldn't that be nice," Marsha said. She gave Jacob a warning glance, then turned to gaze out the window with Mindy.

"Anyway," Arturo said, continuing the conversation they had started hours earlier, "do you think the aliens will take their Dragons and leave us alone?"

"It's hard to say," Jacob answered. "If our theories are correct they'll want to leave enough of everything alive to propagate for their next swing thorough our system. To do anything else would be stupid, not to mention irresponsible. On the other hand, Marsha and I believe our President is going to go after them with everything he has, in which case it's our guess the aliens won't want us around any longer."

"Maybe they'll be benevolent," Marsha said. "Maybe, once they see they've spawned an intelligent species, they'll take us under their wing."

"You keep saying that," Jacob said. "Get real."

"You get real."

"Samuels is going to try and take those things out?" Arturo asked from across the room, where he was setting up his radio equipment. A communications expert, Arturo could reach anywhere in the world if conditions were right. Tomorrow night, if the rains let up and the generator was working properly, he would ask the others to help him relink his equipment to the antenna he had rigged in Jacob's back yard. Luckily it had escaped the Dragon's fury.

"He and his advisors believe it's the only way," Jacob continued. He frowned at Marsha, then looked back to his son-in-law. "They don't believe anyone that consistently rapes a planet like they have our Earth will be benevolent at all. And I know it's cliche, but they're so far ahead of us they'll probably think of us as monkeys, and as competition for their food."

"Can we win such a war?" Tricia asked. She was stroking little Megan's hair, who had come to sit with her, a raggedy Teddy Bear in tow.

"Apparently the President thinks we can," Jacob said. "We've still got nuclear weapons, and so do a lot of other countries. Pappy told us there were thirty-six ships. I'm sure there are more than enough nukes to go around. Our best chance will be surprise and, if the ships come straight in, we should have that."

"*If,*" Marsha said, turning from the window to look at Jacob. "Always 'If.' If they're so far advanced, how can they not know we're here? Our cities on fire, and everything? They must suspect something."

"We can't give up hope, Mom," Tricia said. "If we give that up, then we have nothing."

"But, using nukes will cause a nuclear winter," Arturo objected.

"Yeah," Jacob sighed. "That's the bad part. I don't see anyway around it."

"Then what is the point?"

"The point is nukes may be the lesser of two evils, Art." Jacob said. "It's a tough call. I'm glad I don't have to make it."

"Even if we decide to fight the ships," Arturo said, "how do we do that if we are not sure where they will land?"

"If my theory is correct, we have a pretty good idea on that," Marsha said.

"Yeah," Jacob said. "That narrows it down to only a couple of hundred sites."

* * *

The following night, once the rains had stopped, Arturo and the others hooked up the radio. Once back inside Arturo started the small generator he had brought with him and turned the radio on.

"Last time I listened there were still some stations out there," he said, turning the dials. "The one from Colorado Springs has been broadcasting every hour on the hour. Let's see if they are still there. It is almost eight."

After a few squeaks and squawks Arturo had the station. Sharing the room with the Malfuscos, Tricia, Arturo and the girls were a dozen other people from the neighborhood and beyond. An Asian dentist and his wife, a retired black female school teacher and two tall, muscular construction workers along with their wives and children. Mindy and Megan were overjoyed, as were the Malfuscos. Survivors of the original holocaust, the two brothers carried M-16 rifles, their wives double barreled shotguns, the same weapons that had deterred the attacking Dragon the day before. No one had seen the beast since.

"Not that we've been looking for him," John Robbins, the older of the two brothers, said. The taller of the two, John was still nursing burns along his neck, right shoulder and arm.

"They seem to be territorial animals," Shin Woo, the dentist, added. He and his diminutive, shy wife carried 30-30's. "He was waiting for us at first, when we were stupid enough to go out. We lost a lot of neighbors. The Dragons seem to have partitioned off the city, though they nest together over at the park. What they're eating we don't know. People trying to get out, or scavenging, I guess. Stray animals . . ."

"Listen!" Arturo said, putting a finger to his lips to silence the others. He gestured towards the radio.

". . . while most of Europe appears close to being overrun also," the urgent voice said. "Dragons are already in the heart of Africa, a continent where they have met little resistance. It is feared that once the continent is conquered the invaders will move north into Europe and Arabia, further complicating matters there. The coastal areas of the world are gone. From the news we're getting the Dragons are having a heyday with populations trying to flee inland. Russia and its former inland territories appear to be the only major nations as yet unaffected by the invasion. Interior Canada and the United States, along with South America, are making concentrated stands at certain points with some success, but the Dragons, with reinforcements flying in, are making inroads on all fronts. The islands of the world are gone, although we are still getting sporadic signals from Alice Springs in the heart of Australia . . ."

"Oh, Mom, listen," Tricia said, looking at Marsha, "Alice Springs! We stayed there those three weeks, remember? Good for you, Alice Springs!" Tricia cheered.

" . . . at this rate," the announcer was saying, "it is predicted our planet will be completely overrun in two to three months. Starvation has set in across the planet . . ."

"Turn that damn thing off," John said, standing up from where he had been kneeling by the radio. "Who wants to hear that crap? I can't believe we're not kicking these things' asses. Where the hell is our military?"

"Stretched all over hell and gone," Jacob said. "Way too thin. How do you defend a whole damn continent? And the rest of the world has counted on us to defend them for so long there are relatively few conventional weapons left. Not enough, anyway. We and our allies disarmed the militant nations awhile back, remember? We're the only ones left. Us and Russia, and maybe China and a few European countries. All's that's left are nuclear missiles and a whole lot of Navy ships that are useless on land. We're screwed people, and we might as well get used to it."

John turned the radio down and looked at Jacob. "I don't know about you, mister, but me and my family here ain't licked. And if you are, then, please, be my guest, and get out of this room and go somewhere else."

All eyes turned to Jacob. He put his hands up in surrender.

"Sorry," he said, lowering his arms. "Sorry to all of you. It gets to me, is all. In never lets up. First the eggs, then the oceans, then the Dragons and now the ships. People starving. There's never any good news. It never lets up, is all."

"It gets to all of us," John said, his anger dissipating. "All the more reason we need to stick together here. We, you and I, Jake, and the rest of us, we need to survive. Personally I don't think we were put on this planet to fold at the first real challenge we get. It'll be up to those of us that make it to get humanity back on its feet, to repopulate, and I, for one, intend to survive. There were too many people around anyway. Maybe this is God's way of thinning things out."

"John Robbins!" his wife said, giving him a hard stare.

"All right," Jacob said. He looked around the room. "I stand corrected. Again. But talk is cheap. I suggest we start planning for the worst while hoping for the best."

"Isn't that what we've been doing all along?" Marsha asked.

* * *

Jacob and the rest began to fight a losing battle. Banding together in the late night hours the men and women split into groups and forayed out at night, Marsha staying home with the children in a pre-designated spot, usually someone's basement. They soon found they had competition. In mid-October they traveled over a mile and a half away, having depleted their immediate neighborhood of anything edible. The night was cool and windy, with a full moon making the broken landscape much too dangerous. Foraging like rats over rough terrain, their hearts pounding with every new sound, Jacob and John, along with John's wife Hannah and their sixteen-year-old son Mark, found themselves the victims of shots being fired. No one was hit, but a warning came down from a tall, burned-out building overlooking several square miles.

"Stay out!" an angry voice yelled. "Stay out of our territory! You set foot over here again and we'll shoot to kill!"

Not wanting a confrontation, and not knowing who they were up against, Jacob's group of hungry scavengers beat a hasty retreat. Water and food for eighteen souls became increasingly scarce as the days crept by. Word filtered in that five young people from a neighboring tribe had been killed one night, ambushed by a pair of Dragons while crossing a street.

"They have learned to hunt together," a despairing Arturo said upon hearing the news. "And an ambush, no less. What are we to do now? There will be Dragons around every corner."

"It's definitely an improvement in their thought processes," Jacob said, equally depressed. "If their brains are still evolving we won't stand a chance."

"We don't know that, Dad," Tricia said, looking for a ray of hope. "Maybe the two just happened to be in the same place at the same time. Maybe they're getting hungry enough now to invade each other's territory. Maybe the damn things will start eating each other if they get hungry enough."

"Or fly away and leave us alone," Marsha said.

"Wishful thinking, all of you. And you know it," Jacob said.

Despite their best efforts the group became increasingly desperate as each day passed, their spirits eroding with each new sunrise and sunset. All their water was now collected from rainfall, which was never enough and had to be rationed. What would happen next summer, when the rains quit? How were they going to eat without scavenging outside their territory? Without taking the risk of being killed by one of their own kind? It was a miserable, cowardly time, and the rest or the world fared the same, or worse.

"They have overrun most of Europe and India," Arturo told a somber group of half-starved people in mid-November. "They are inside of Russia, and deep into China and the Middle East. South America and Canada have quit reporting. Apparently, along with Russia and the Chinese, our country is one of the last lines of defense. Which makes sense, since we have all of the weapons. We are still alive from Santa Fe, New Mexico north to Casper, Wyoming, and east to Oklahoma City, Wichita, Kansas and North Platte, Nebraska, then west to Grand Junction, Colorado. A rough rectangle. Except for a few strays the interior has not been penetrated. What is left of our ground defenses have set up perimeters around what cities we have left. Unfortunately, once the Dragons deplete their local food sources they join up with the others on the perimeters. There are more Dragons on our borders than ever before. According to the announcer our ground and air forces seem to be holding up for now. That is the upside, anyway."

"Upside?" Jacob questioned. "Then what the hell is the downside?"

"You mean besides the fact that we are running out of ammunition, gas and things like that?"

"Yeah. Things like that."

"Well, from what I am hearing, there are roughly fifty million or so Americans packed into that little rectangle. There is very little food and medicine, let alone enough shelter, and winter has already started and, as you know, winters are very cold in these areas. There are reports of the military firing on the civilians, and the civilians are firing back. It is a real mess."

"So what else is new?" Jacob said sarcastically.

"Dear God," Marsha said, looking out the basement window. "What's to become of us?"

"It's gotten down to every man for himself, then," Tricia said.

"Oh, I think it was down to that a long time ago," Marsha said, turning to look at her daughter. She watched, a cup of weak tea in hand, as Mindy got up from beside her and walked towards the makeshift kitchen. Seven pounds lighter than when they'd first found her, Mindy was fast becoming unable to function normally, as was the rest of the group.

"I'm hungry," she said, poking around in some empty wooden boxes. Everyone else was hungry too, but nobody echoed the fact. Marsha, fifteen pounds lighter than she had been a month ago, got up to see what she could find.

John Robbins, who had lost twenty pounds, most of it muscle, got up from where he had been sitting and took Marsha's spot by the window. Holding on tight to his M-16 he looked out and around.

"Maybe it's time we organized a Dragon hunt," he said, his jaw set. He turned back to face the others. "Change the order of things a little. Personally, I'm getting tired of sitting around on my ass all of the time."

"Me too," Nick, his younger brother, echoed.

"What are you talking about?" Hannah, John's wife, asked. "Have you guys gone daffy? You'll just be another meal for the damn things. I don't like that idea at all."

"I have to admit I have been thinking the same thing," Arturo said from his seat by Tricia. "We can do that, or sit here and slowly starve. Not only that, I am getting so white sitting inside all of the time that my relatives will not know it is me when they see me again!"

Jacob spoke when everyone had finished laughing.

"And how do you plan on doing this, John?" he asked. "We know they nest in Balboa Park, and that there's about a dozen of them at any given time. It would be sheer suicide to go in there."

"I've given it a lot of thought, Jake. What else is there to do? The thing is, we're going to reach a point pretty soon where we'll be ineffective as hunters, we'll be too weak, and I'm not ready to play cannibal. Now, if you'll all gather 'round, here's what I'm thinking. First of all, we'll need to enlist help from some of our neighbors. Second, we'll need some bait. Live, human bait . . ."

Chapter 26
Desperate Measures

Two days later the battleground was set. After some lengthy white-flag discussions with several neighboring groups, Robbins' plan was agreed to, but only after John and Nick had volunteered to be the bait. Shortly after noon on a clear, crisp fall day, the plan was put into action.

"All set?" John asked Jacob from a second story bedroom. They were three houses down from where the Malfuscos and their group lived. In case the plan backfired Jacob didn't want his new home flattened as his old one had been.

"I guess so," Jacob said nervously, one of Robbins' deer rifles in hand. "You sure you want to do this?"

"I don't want to do it, Jake, but I got no choice. None of us do. You okay with that rifle?"

"No."

"You'll do fine. Aim for his eyes on the downswing, and his ass hole on the upswing. Just don't hit me or Nick."

Jacob nodded. He looked across Georgia Street, then up and down. He couldn't see the people in the houses and apartment buildings, but knew there were twenty-nine men, women and children perched behind second, third and fourth story windows. All armed with deer rifles, or better.

"You think those guys with the bazooka can hit anything?" Jacob asked as John made ready to go downstairs.

"They say they can."

"But they're just kids!"

"It's their bazooka. And they say they've fired it before."

"At what?"

John shrugged.

"Great. If they can't shoot the damn thing then we're all dead."

"What time you got?"

"Five to three."

"Got to go, Jake. You'll do as you promised? Look after Hannah and the kids if something happens to me and Nick?"

"I said I would."

"All right," John said. He extended his hand, which Jacob shook, then headed downstairs. After John had disappeared Jacob took his position at the window. His heart increased its beat, his hands began to tremble and thin lines of sweat trickled down his face.

* * *

"All set?" John asked his brother once he had his shotgun in hand.

"Yeah," Nick said from where the two huddled beneath the overhang of a small porch. "But I still don't see why some of these other guys can't come along. Bunch of fricking cowards you ask me."

"It was our idea, Nick. Maybe we're hungrier than they are. Be thankful they agreed to it."

"Yeah, but . . ."

"Still not too late to back out, little bro."

"Yeah? Then who's gonna protect your scrawny ass, John? None of these other guys volunteered."

"Then shut up and let's go."

* * *

Two minutes later the men were out on Georgia Street, in plain sight, gazing into the late afternoon sun. Both carried shotguns, feeling rifles at close range would do them little good.

"What if no one comes?" Nick asked as the two men began pacing up and down the street.

"It'll come," John said, biting at his nails. "It may take awhile, but it will come. They have to eat, too."

"What if there's more than one?"

* * *

Seven long, nervous minutes later the sun was eclipsed as a huge, winged shape flew in from the southwest. A loud screeching pierced the air, and panic filled the hearts of twenty-nine starved and desperate human beings.

"Run!" John screamed at Nick as the Dragon veered closer.

"Damn," Jacob muttered as he fumbled with the bolt on his rifle. His hands fairly shook now as he brought the sights to bear. Up and down Georgia Street and across it others took aim.

On the street below Nick Robbins froze in his tracks. John, on the run, dove and rolled beneath an armored truck as planned. Shots began barking from the windows. First one, then another, then a series of rapid-fire volleys. Still Nick did not move. Jacob fired, the impact of the recoil knocking him backwards. John peered out from beneath the truck in time to see his brother plucked from the street like a trout from a lake. A loud roar exploded into the air as the bazooka was fired, missing its mark by fifty feet and ripping apart the fifth story of an unoccupied office building a quarter mile up the street. A bullet hit the Dragon's right rear kneecap, temporarily causing the muscles there to lose their tension. Enough damage was done that the Dragon lost its grip and dropped Nick back onto the street. He hit on his side, bounced once and lay still, blood oozing from his head and where the Dragon had grabbed him about the shoulders. Several errant bullets shattered glass over Jacob's head, blew holes in the wall and sent him huddling to the floor.

"Damn!" he muttered, getting back up in time to fire a last shot at the retreating Dragon. Down below John rolled out from under the truck and stumbled towards his brother, now a good one hundred and fifty feet up the street.

"Shit," Jacob cursed. He turned from the window and ran downstairs, dropping his weapon in the process. Soon he was in the street, angling towards Nick. The Dragon flapped its wings and veered left, skimming several apartment roof tops as it rose into the air. Shots rang out. The Dragon circled and headed back in, its screeching angry and defiant. Jacob ran and tackled John from behind. Both men fell in a heap and rolled on the rough cement.

"Don't be stupid!" Jacob yelled as John broke his grasp and got up. The air was once again filed with heavy rifle fire as the Dragon, bleeding from several wounds, tilted its thirty-foot wings and flapped to a stop, landing not twenty yards upstreet from Nick. More firing of rifles mingled with the frightening thud of bullets as they ricocheted into surrounding vehicles and buildings. The Dragon let out a terrible roar. Rearing on its hind legs and using its tail for balance, the beast strained its body and craned its neck, breathing fire onto the buildings to its immediate right. Apartment houses and homes exploded and burst into flames. Men, women and children screamed. The Dragon turned its attention to the other side of the street and did the same. More buildings burst into flames. Two men ran from one of the houses, their clothing on fire. The air was filled with another tremendous roar as the Dragon fell back to its front feet. Shaking its head and screeching the Dragon walked over the unconscious Nick and on past for another thirty yards, then reared on its hind legs and began spitting fire all over again. Jacob and John were already on the run when a stream of flaming gas scorched trees and shrubs to their left. From the basement of an apartment building to their right two teenaged boys suddenly appeared. With shaking hands and bodies they positioned themselves and aimed their bazooka.

"Keep running!" John yelled as he looked over his shoulder at the fire belching monster.

"No shit!" Jacob yelled above the din. Both men came to an alleyway and bore into it. Jacob stumbled, fell and got back up. The boys could barely miss so huge a target at such close range, but they almost did. With a loud "WHUMP" the shell left its casing, hit the Dragon on the inside of its right rear leg and detonated. Flesh and blood exploded onto the street and the surrounding buildings. The Dragon fell heavily onto its right side, twitching violently. It tried to get up, then fell again, screeching from its pain. Giving up it lay relatively still, its sides heaving as it struggled to stay alive. Blood poured into the street and ran down the gutter.

Upon hearing the explosion Jacob and John stopped running. Both men turned and hurried back to the corner.

"It's down!" Jacob exclaimed. "The kids got it with their bazooka!"

"Then let's go!" John said. "We've got no time to lose. There may be others close by."

Both men ran to where the Dragon lay. John ran on past, barely glancing at the beast as he hurried towards his brother, still unconscious on the pavement. Jacob stopped and surveyed the Dragon, several yards away, along with the two boys who had fired the bazooka, neither of whom looked older than fifteen. Both were staring wide eyed at the huge, panting creature before them. All three kept a healthy distance.

Soon, except for four women who went to look after the burned men, they were joined by the rest of the alliance. Seconds passed before Jacob summoned enough courage to move closer to the Dragon. Large, slanted, baleful eyes watched him as he crept forward. Jacob glanced into those deep, yellow pools and was mysteriously moved. His insides turned and for an instant he felt a kinship with the Dragon, much as men feel a kinship with lions and tigers. Then, as quickly as the feeling had come, it was gone. The beast's chest rattled, Jacob heard a final wheezing and the Dragon stopped its twitching. Silent for a moment, Jacob shook off his emotions and moved into action.

"All right, let's get moving!" he commanded of the others. "You know the plan. Move your rear, get your gear and start cutting! Pass the word. And be quick! There's no telling how long we have before the other Dragons discover what's going on here."

Up the street John had dodged pieces of flaming debris and chunks of concrete in reaching his brother. On either side of Georgia Street houses and apartments were in flames. Smoke billowed into the air. A charred body lay on the sidewalk, having fallen from above. John gathered Nick in his arms and carried him towards Jacob's new quarters, there to be greeted by Marsha, Nick's wife and two wide-eyed little girls, anxious to help where they could. Others went to work butchering the Dragon.

* * *

Later that evening Jacob and his family huddled in the basement. Their grizzly task accomplished his allies in arms, loaded down with Dragon meat, had gone back to their homes. The various groups, for all intents and purposes, were enemies once again. Outside a half dozen starving Dragons fought over the remains of their dead kin. The street rumbled with their weight as they hopped about, flapping their wings and screeching like vultures over a road kill. Plaster and strings of insulation fell from the ceiling as the house shook, and shook again.

"It is like an earthquake that does not end," Arturo complained well into the evening. "Lucky for us they are well down the street."

"Yeah. Lucky us," Jacob said.

Over in a corner of the room a semiconscious Nick Robbins lay on one of the beds, tended to by his wife Maggie along with Hannah and Doctor Woo, all of whom had elected to spend the night, and had been welcomed to do so. Despite a broken arm, multiple bruises, a slight concussion and several holes in his shoulders, Nick was holding his own.

"Takes more than no damn Dragon to kill *my* brother," John said proudly, though badly shaken from the days events. He stood with Jacob, Marsha, Tricia, Arturo, Mindy and Dorothy Woo at a makeshift butcher's table, cutting large chunks of red meat into smaller ones. When done they would cook and salt the meat for later use, having already had their fill of the raw stuff. They had been that hungry.

"Strange," Jacob muttered once their work was about done, still disturbed by his meeting with the Dragon.

"What's that, dear?" Marsha asked, finishing up. She wiped bloody hands on a towel she had wrapped around her waist.

"When I looked into its eyes, the Dragon's eyes, I'd swear it was asking me to help it. I had a dog once, when I was a kid. A beautiful collie. We called him Biscuit. Lived almost fourteen years, he did. When he lay dying Old Biscuit would look at me with those sad eyes and I could tell he was asking me what was the matter? Why was he in such pain? Had he done something wrong? Why wasn't I helping him? I swear that creature from hell had the same helpless look in its eyes. A sort of pleading. An innocence, if you will. God help me, I actually felt sorry for it."

"C'mon, Jake," John said from Nick's bedside, holding his brother's hand. "The damn thing has killed a lot of people. Four today, if you've forgotten, and it almost killed my brother."

"I know, John. I'm just saying."

Chapter 27
Earth's End

By December tenth two-thirds of Earth's human population had perished, and the other one third was in imminent danger of following suit. Hundreds of thousands were dying each day, falling prey to the Dragons, or dying of starvation, thirst, disease or exposure. Some fell prey to their fellow man, so overpowering was the hunger that ravaged the planet. The Dragons continued to grow, both in size and intelligence. They became more formidable, and their appetites were insatiable. Then, with humanity on the brink of annihilation, when the United States' last line of defense was in danger of collapsing and the rest of the world lay in ruins, the Dragons withdrew.

"They're gone?" a thin and subdued Jack Samuels asked from his retreat well within Cheyenne Mountain. Outside a hard, wind-driven snow was falling and a city overflowing with humanity tried to keep warm and find something to eat. Despite all the military's hoarding of foodstuffs there was not much left. People subsisted on Dragon meat, when they could get it, along with rats, mice, beetles, moldy corn and used coffee grounds. "Where did they go?"

"They've migrated back to the coastlines, as best we can tell," a haggard General Walter Taffey said. "Along the sands and jetties where they first came ashore. They seem to be, well, hibernating. That's the best description I can think of. Not moving around much. You know, like bears in winter?"

"But why?" Samuels asked.

"We think they're conserving energy. Hoarding their fat, as it were. Waiting for their masters to come and get them."

"Then they're sitting ducks!"

"They would be if we had anything left to fight them with," a defeated and haggard General Cable said from across the table. "What reserves we have are here, protecting us, or at designated outposts, dug in and waiting for the ships to land."

"You're talking about our nuclear weapons."

"Yes, sir."

Samuels got up and walked around the room, his head down. He scrutinized his military advisors and cabinet members, those that were left, those had not gone home to try and find their families. Those that remained watched as their President circled the conference room table, his head down. Twice around and Samuels slumped back in his chair.

"All this time and there's still something I don't understand," he said, looking to Cable. "How are these things able to survive on our planet? First the oceans, then the land. Everything I ever read on creatures from outer space is their metabolism would be different from ours. Their air would be different, their food, their blood, all that. Yet here they are, in a supposedly hostile environment, and they're thriving. I don't understand."

"I can shed some light on that, Jack," Cina Chang said from down the table.

"Go on."

"We believe they've been genetically altered, boss. In fact, our scientists are positive on the matter. They're telling us that Dragon metabolism is the same as ours, and their DNA is structured almost exactly as ours is. I'm talking about all life on Earth, Jack, and not specifically human DNA."

"I still don't understand."

"These Dragons, their ancestors, we believe they originated on Earth, Jack. Millions and millions of years ago. As dinosaurs."

* * *

"Who has the update on their ships?" Samuels asked after a while, after he and the others had mulled over what Chang had said.

"They're about two weeks away," Cable answered.

Samuels nodded. "And our defenses are ready? Our missiles?" His eyes fell on Admiral Peronski.

"Our ships are positioned all around the globe, Mr. President . . ."

"Damn it, Roland!" Samuels barked. "Would you call me Jack, like I asked you to? There's nothing to be President of anymore, or have you forgotten?"

"As you wish, sir," Peronski said, too tired to argue. "As I was saying, our ships are positioned on the insight Mrs. Malfusco gave us awhile back. The other countries, those that still have a navy, are there, right beside us. Russia and Ukraine, plus a few other countries, still have functional silos on land. Even so, with all the possible landing sights, we can't cover them all. And then there's . . ."

"Roland! Are we ready?"

"As ready as we'll ever be, sir."

"Thank you! At least we have some idea of where they might land. That gives us a chance," Samuels said. He glanced towards a map of the world hanging on the west wall, a map with little red flags pinned all over it.

"Do you still plan on using nuclear weapons, Jack?" Wanda Grayfeather, seated across from Chang, asked.

"We'll do what we have to do."

"I don't agree."

"I know."

"What good will it do? We've agreed there is an outside chance they will leave us alone, maybe even apologize and take us under their wing. If we nuke them then the whole world goes. Where's the logic in that?"

"You want us to give up our home without a fight?"

"We've *been* fighting, Jack."

"Wanda, when you're at war, and retreating, you try not to leave the enemy anything he can work with. Apparently these aliens have been raping our world for millions of years. Other worlds too, as we've discussed. It's time we put a stop to it, one way or another. At least here."

"By sterilizing our whole planet?"

"We're betting we won't be sterilizing everything, Wanda."

"That's a bet you'll lose, Jack, and you know it. I must protest this action in the strongest terms possible. And I'm not alone!"

"You're protest is duly noted, Wanda. I'm sorry. Now, let's move on here . . . ."

Chapter 28
Winter Solstice

Arturo gave Marsha the news on the morning of December sixteenth.

"I knew it!" Marsha exclaimed. "I've always known it, but nobody ever listened. Get me the President!"

* * *

What remained of the world's once formidable military might watched and waited as the invading ships entered the Earth's atmosphere on December twenty-first. After having spent the prior day orbiting, they descended deliberately, and slowly. Huge, rectangular, blue-gray vessels, a mile across, two miles long and forty stories high, homing in on ancient beacons buried thousands of years ago.

"Why rectangular?" Samuels asked, his nerves as tight as a bowstring. He watched the ships orbit, then separate and descend.

"My guess is for efficiency of space," Martin Davis answered. "They're factory ships, after all. At least that's what we think they are. Ugly goddam things if you ask me."

"I feel like I'm in a dream," Samuels said. He watched spellbound as instrumentation and TVs around the room tracked the ships. Computers clicked and clacked. Missiles around the world were given last minute instructions by sweating personnel.

"More like a fucking nightmare," Aaron Cable said.

* * *

The alien ships reached their destinations at approximately the same time. Once there they maneuvered above their targets for minutes, then stopped dead in the air. There were no visible signs of anything holding them up. No sound could be heard, no flashing light seen, no turrets, projections, bumps or bulges. Nothing. Just enormous, sleek, six-sided boxes hanging in the air. They rested, if that was the proper term, above Easter Island, Stonehenge and the Egyptian pyramids. Above Uluru, Death Valley, Babylon, Mojenjo-Daro, Pedra Pinata, Tiahuanaco, the Chulala pyramid, Kunming, Oppama, Yonaguni and Delhi. Shensi, Hawaii, Tassili, Uzbekistan, Nazca. The Canary Islands, Zimbabwe, Glozel, Baalbek, Knosos-Minoa, Mystery Hill and where Atlantis used to be. Rio de Janeiro and other places no one ever suspected they would visit.

"I told you," Marsha said, overwhelmed that her predictions were coming true. "It confirms what I, and others, have said all along. These places they're hovering over all jive with the winter solstice somehow. Humanity was jump started at all these places. I knew it. Others knew it. But nobody listened. And we've never been able to figure out why. Now everyone knows."

"Yeah, that does everyone a lot of good," Jacob said, a thought echoed by others in the room. Weak and miserable others, others who'd had nothing to eat for several days. "I don't see humanity getting slaughtered as anything to cheer about."

"I never heard you mention Death Valley before, Mom," Tricia said from where she lay on a bed in the corner, fighting weakness. A candle glowed beside her, one of two lighting an otherwise dark room. Outside it was even darker, and welcome rain pelted down. Trash cans, buckets and other containers, placed in strategic locations, collected all they could. Hopefully there would be enough for small baths, something the group hadn't had in weeks. The basement roof leaked and water was seeping in through the concrete walls. It was a cold, damp and miserable time, and people becoming sick could only think they might get sicker.

"I'm sure, darling," Marsha said, gazing into the darkness with a cup of sugared, hot water in hand, "that if we ever get the chance we'll find a Stonehenge or a pyramid buried there, just like we did at Uluru. Those places are beacons. Beacons built into the Earth that our forefathers erected monuments over to worship their space faring gods."

* * *

"The world is waiting on your orders, Jack," General Cable said from his station at NORAD'S command headquarters inside Cheyenne Mountain.

"Only three ships have landed in the United States?" Samuels asked, his heart pounding. Even though the room was cool he was sweating, running a fever. Not feeling well, Samuels was worried about having a heart attack. Aided by a glass of water, he swallowed a series of pills his personal physician had prescribed.

"They haven't exactly landed, sir. They're still in limbo, at five hundred feet up."

"They haven't fired on anything or done any damage? No side doors have opened with little green men walking down gold plated ramps? No attack planes flying out?"

"No, sir. Just sitting there in mid air."

"All right," Samuels said, sitting down. He wiped at his brow with a well used handkerchief. "Let's hold our fire. Call the others and ask them to do the same. Beg them if you have to. Maybe our visitors are going to leave us alone."

"Damn it, Jack," Cable said. "If we wait until *they* fire there won't be any of *us* left to retaliate!"

"And damn it, Aaron, I know that!" Samuels said. He glanced around at his demoralized staff. "Let's not forget that we're in damn poor shape to wage a battle right now. If any of you think we have even the slightest chance against these, these people then I suggest you retool your thinking. They don't fire on us, we don't fire on them. That's my decision."

"The rest of the world may not follow suit, Jack," Admiral Peronski said.

"The rest of the world be damned. I'm going next door and get some sleep. Wake me if anything extraordinary occurs."

"Alien space ships on our doorstep and he wants to sleep?" General Jackson said after Samuels had exited the room.

"Yeah. I wonder what the hell 'anything extraordinary' is supposed to mean?" Cable said. Others in the room could only look his way and shake their heads.

* * *

At precisely noon, Greenwich time, on the twenty-first of December, a high pitched wailing began to emit from the ships. Sleeping Dragons unfurled their wings and flew uneasily to the vessels calling them. Great sliding doors in the belly of each ship opened and invited them in. The world, those people that were left and able, watched in awe as the huge, winged beasts, those not seriously wounded or otherwise detained, migrated north and south, east and west, unable to ignore the signals that beckoned them to their deaths.

* * *

"They're leaving!" Arturo shouted from atop a twelve story, burned out apartment house, a place he and the others had established to keep an eye out for Dragons, and intruders. "The news was correct. Come and look!"

Jacob, Marsha and Mindy hurried across the sun-dappled street and up the rebuilt stairs to the top of the building. They were just in time to see ten of the beasts rise from the park and join thousands of others heading east, lambs being led to the slaughter. Their forlorn screeching filled the air, and pierced the hearts of those watching.

"They're really quite beautiful, in their own way," Marsha said, her mouth open, as the Dragons cried out and veered north, towards Death Valley. "I kind of wish, well, I wish I had known them better, you know?"

"Yeah, me too," Jacob said.

"You two are kidding me here, right?" Arturo said.

* * *

"Are they gone?" A weary, yet jubilant, President Samuels asked the following day. "They just up and left?"

"Yes, sir," Cable answered. "All the ships headed back into space less than twenty minutes ago."

"And the Dragons with them?"

"As far as we know, sir. I'm sure there'll be stragglers, like there were before. Shouldn't take long to hunt them down and rid our planet of the bastards. Don't need any reminders roaming around."

"No," Samuels said. "Let's don't do that. Make plans to save any stragglers, any wounded or whatever. I'm sure our scientists will want to study them. Our people may not like it at first, but they'll come around. Am I understood here?"

"Yes, sir," Cable said. "I'll issue the order."

The President looked around the room, at the relieved faces of his hastily gathered advisors, Joint Chiefs of Staff and Cabinet members. He had a lot of questions on his mind.

"Anybody want to tell me their ideas on why these ships left without incident?" he asked, glancing around the room.

"I can answer that, Jack," Dr. Jeremy Craft, his tall, lanky, top science advisor, answered. "We were able to take heat scans of two of their ships from two of our Carriers, one stationed off the coast of California, west of

Death Valley, and the other off the east coast near Mystery Hill, in New England. We were able to do this before the Dragons were called on board. As far as we can tell there were no life forms aboard those ships, Mr. President. None at all."

"What are you saying?"

"They were drones, Jack. Robot ships. We don't have confirmation from all the nations, yet, but we believe all their vessels were the same."

"But, wouldn't the aliens know that we'd killed off half their food supply, and want to take revenge?" Samuels asked. "I mean, surely they must have pictures, or something, of what went on here. Seems to me they should have some concern, good or bad, that we have cities and missiles and things like that. It doesn't make sense that they would just come, and leave, does it? Don't they care?"

"We're sure they know, Mr. President," Craft continued, having the attention of the entire room. "As you know we still have people at Palomar. They've assured us that the three alien suns and their ring worlds are continuing on their journey out of our solar system, and the factory ships are on trajectory to join them. The suns have neither increased, or decreased, their speed since we discovered them, Jack. As sophisticated as their technology is, I don't think they have the resources to slow their suns down so they can take a better look at us. And we don't think they have the money to send back war ships, either. They must have economics, like we do. They sent their robot ships to Earth knowing they would be up against an emerging civilization, but apparently they could care less. Nobody's out to get *them*. Not only that, I think the cost of their coming back here now would be prohibitive. They're moving away too fast. In any case, I guess we'll find out in the coming days. They got what they came for. Some of it, anyway."

"You think they might still come back?" Samuels asked wearily.

"Anything's possible sir, but, personally, I doubt it."

Samuels nodded. "Got any world news, Marty?" he asked his Chief of Staff.

"Some good and some bad, Jack. We're figuring we've lost close to eighty percent of Earth's human population, and we'll lose more until we can get back on our feet. The poorer nations have suffered the most, as was expected. But there are some good signs."

"Go on."

"Apparently our oceans are already regenerating. Our Navy has reported seeing an abundance of small fish swimming in close to shore, and in estuaries and the like. As has been mentioned before, the world's phytoplankton weren't harmed by the invasion, nor our zooplankton either. With few large fish left to graze on them, they're thriving. And it's our guess, at this point in time, that those egg shells the juvenile Dragons arrived in released additional nutrients into our oceans, designed to help just such a rejuvenation."

"That is good news," Samuels said, managing a slight smile. "Anything else?"

"Our cities, the cities of the world, they're destroyed, sir."

"I'm aware of that, Jeremy. What's your point?"

"Before, when the Dragons invaded, they faced no enemies and all the land was open, unobstructed. They did their nasty business and moved on through, leaving the land to regenerate, much the same as the oceans. But now, with concrete covering most of our world's prime land, and our planet's ecology already in peril before they landed . . . well, sir, I'm sure you get the picture."

"We have a lot of work to do," Samuels said.

"Yes, sir."

"I've got one last question, then we'll take a break and get something to eat," Samuels said. "What I don't understand is that these people must have paid us a visit last time they were here. To plant their beacons, or whatever, and to give the human race its 'Jump Start,' if our theories are correct. They had to have built that pyramid at Uluru, remember? Since they showed up the last time they were here, why not this time? Surely they would want to know if their experiment worked or not."

"May I?" Wanda Grayfeather asked, raising her hand.

"By all means," Samuels answered.

"They have been here, Jack," Wanda started. "Flying saucers, alien abductions, Roswell, New Mexico. They've been here all right, and relatively recently, which would coincide with all else that has happened."

"Yet they sent their Dragons, knowing full well we had the capability to destroy them."

"But we didn't destroy them, Jack. They may have sent 'extras' to compensate. And they weren't too worried about our 'capability.' We only have to look around to see that. We pretty much destroyed our own planet without them firing a single shot. With these facts in hand I think it's safe to say they're a pretty callous bunch. Weigh the evidence. They could care less whether we survived or not. They've ruled the universe for so long we're probably no more than piss ants on sugar to them."

"If that's true, Wanda, then they've made a mistake. I think we'll have a big surprise in store for them the next time they visit. Better yet, it wouldn't surprise me if we're not out there hunting them down in a hundred years or so. They'll wish the hell they never saw us in the first place. Perhaps this will help bring humans together for once, with a common enemy to fight. Now that would be a surprise, huh?"

"One other thing, Jack."

Samuels looked at his watch. His stomach growled. "You have one minute, Wanda."

"A lot of people have always thought that, were it not for the asteroid that all but wiped out the dinosaurs those millions of years ago, that one of their species would one day have developed intelligence and ruled the Earth."

"Go on."

"These Dragons, Jack. They are that species."

Chapter 29
Eight Months Later

The Malfuscos sat on their deck, beneath a tattered umbrella, and watched as the late summer sun rippled the surface of their pool. Crickets chirped somewhere in the lawn. A thermometer hanging on the wall of their house registered a scorching 101 degrees in the shade.

"Damn, it's hot here," Marsha said, fanning herself with an old magazine, one she'd read a dozen times. "Why would anyone want to live in Fresno?"

"*We're* living here."

"I said *'Want to'*, Malfunction."

"Jump in the pool, " Jacob said, leaning back in his recliner. Trim and bronze, both the Malfuscos were forty pounds lighter than when they had first met. They were lean and mean, as Jacob liked to say. Farm work in the heat, not to mention barely enough food to get by, did that to you.

"Maybe we can go back to San Diego when the harvest is done," Marsha said. "See how the old town is faring. Santa Monica, too. Cooler there, by the sea."

"There's nobody there anymore, baby. Just the military and a few civilians working for them. No grocery stores, gas stations, restaurants, shopping malls. It's a dead town. All the west coast cities are dead towns. East coast cities, too. You know that. They have no water, no power, no nothing."

"I don't care. I want to go back! I'd like to cool off, to see the ocean."

"All right! Geez. I'll talk to the general, see if it's okay."

Marsha grunted, then spoke. "Do you think we'll ever recover?" she asked, already planning the trip in her mind. She swatted at a mosquito on her arm. Spanish music floated by from the only other undamaged house on the street. A fat robin hunted in the grass, one of several the Malfuscos had seen since moving to the neighborhood three months ago.

"Eventually," Jacob said, sipping from an iced tea. "Most of America's people are here in the valley now, and in the warmer, southern states, working the farms, taking care of the parentless children. This is a good place. Fresno county used to be the farm production capital of the world. There's plenty of water here, and we've restored the power. It's our breadbasket. The whole

San Joaquin valley is. We'll be all right. And if America is all right, so is the rest of the world."

"I hope so."

"I've been reading up. Did you know, before the Dragons came, that California alone had more gross product than all but four nations in the world? This valley is the most productive farming land in the world, sweetheart. Hot as it is, it's the natural place to start over, for America to get back on its feet. Hell, the President and his staff are right up the street in Sacramento. We'll move back to the Denvers and Chicagos some day, but I couldn't tell you when. Not in our lifetimes. Those of us here are the keys to keeping humanity from sliding back into the dark ages. The rest of the world may not like it, but it's true. Frankly, I'm proud to be here, to be a part of mankind's resurrection, so to speak. Even if it is a hundred degrees all the time."

"I hope we can go home soon," Marsha said wistfully, ignoring Jacob's speech. "Maybe Art and Tricia can go with us, and bring the baby."

Jacob sighed and looked at his watch. A cooling breeze curled across the patio.

"Once the crops are in, we have to go back to teaching, you know that," he said.

"I know."

"Well, we still have time to go and see our resident Dragon," Jacob said, changing the subject, "before they ship him off to the compound in Oregon. Apparently the poor guy is on his feet again, and his wings have mended. If I remember right the zoo will be open until midnight in honor of the occasion. Plus the colonel in charge is supposed to have news on when the government is planning on bringing our people back from the moon and Mars."

"Sounds good to me," Marsha said, jumping to her feet. "I'll get the girls ready and we'll be off."

Chapter 30
Yokosuka, Japan

The two old men stood in the street and looked towards the bay, at the crowd of people there.

"She will be rich and famous one day," Kiego said.

"I think Myoko is already there," Hiro said. "Even with our country destroyed and everyone struggling, she is making money."

The two watched awhile longer before their wrinkled and wizened faces broke into wide grins. They cheered along with others as Myoko and Fujisan rose into the air and headed north towards Tokyo, their precious cargo of freight and passengers on board.

The End

THE FIRE THAT NASA NEVER HAD
by Colonel B. Dean Smith

This book is an account of Colonel B. Dean Smith's flying activities in support of research and development of the United States' Ballistic Missile program and the space exploration of NASA from Cape Canaveral (Kennedy), Florida. Included is a report of a test done for NASA that examined space suits for the Gemini project. During this project, the author and another pilot experienced a disastrous fire in a simulator containing 100% oxygen, nearly taking both their lives. Five years later, in 1967, NASA's Apollo I capsule was consumed by a similar 100% oxygen fire, taking the lives of three astronauts, Gus Grissom, Ed White and Roger Chaffee. The author takes the reader through an account of the preparations made before his test flight and fire. He then makes a comparison of the two fires and the subsequent NASA investigation report of the Apollo I incident and draws conclusions regarding the lessons learned.

Paperback, 270 pages
6" x 9"
ISBN 1-4241-2574-X

About the author:

Colonel B. Dean Smith graduated from the US Naval Academy in 1953, commissioned in the Air Force. After pilot training, he served numerous flying tours and administrative positions. He earned an MBA from GW University, and served a tour in Vietnam, retiring from the Joint Chiefs of Staff on July 1, 1974.

also available from publishamerica

THE BRIDES' FAIR
by Hal Fleming

A novel of international intrigue and terrorism.

The Brides' Fair, an annual folkloric event in the Mid Atlas Mountains of North Africa, serves as an exotic setting for a novel of international intrigue and terrorism. Americans, mountain Berbers, Moroccan Arabs and those of a rebel faction converge on the festival, and it soon becomes clear that their fates are interwoven. The plot is driven by attempts to forestall an act of terrorism, while sub-plots tell of the tangled love interests of the Americans; the frantic efforts of a young Berber girl to escape a forced marriage; the trials of local officials in dealing with threats to their country's national security; and the obstacles faced by a small band of terrorists in carrying out their mission to disrupt the fair. A major disaster is averted at the last minute with the revelation that one giving aid to the terrorists was an American of the diplomatic community.

Paperback, 212 pages
6" x 9"
ISBN 1-60563-706-8

About the author:

Hal Fleming has been a senior official with the Peace Corps, the Department of State, UNICEF and the US Mission to the United Nations. He has lived ten years in West and North Africa. Early on, he worked at Forbes Inc. and taught at the university level. He has published various works and holds degrees from Brown and Columbia.

available to all bookstores nationwide.
www.publishamerica.com

HOVERDOWN

by Raland J. Patterson

Hoverdown is a revenge-driven thriller tracking the lives of three men. Beginning in Vietnam, a skilled helicopter pilot, Bill Dant, foolishly accepts an opportunity to deal drugs to his fellow soldiers. Platoon leader Captain Sam Wright is instrumental in sending him to prison. After three inmates crush his hand, ending any hope of flying again, Dant begins his trail of vengeance. Killing comes as naturally to him as breathing. Captain Wright is disabled by a gunshot wound and goes to work for Jim Coleman, a former self-proclaimed vigilante. After the execution of his wife for a murder he committed, Coleman seeks peace by becoming a lawyer advocating justice for juveniles. A strong-willed doctor, Amanda Hicks, knows she has found a man to reckon with when Coleman refuses to cater to her bossiness and throws her in the lake. The three men's stories merge into a conclusion of startling destiny.

Paperback, 276 pages
6" x 9"
ISBN 1-60474-283-6

About the author:

Raland J. Patterson is a retired Army lieutenant colonel with twenty-two years of active duty. He served in Vietnam as a helicopter pilot from 1970-1971. His awards include the Distinguished Flying Cross, Bronze Star, and fourteen air medals. His second career was as a financial planner in Europe.